GREAT BRITISH HORROR V

MIDSUMMER EVE

Great British Horror V

Midsummer Eve

Edited by

Steve J Shaw

First published in Great Britain in 2020 by

Black Shuck Books
Kent, UK

978-1-913038-62-5

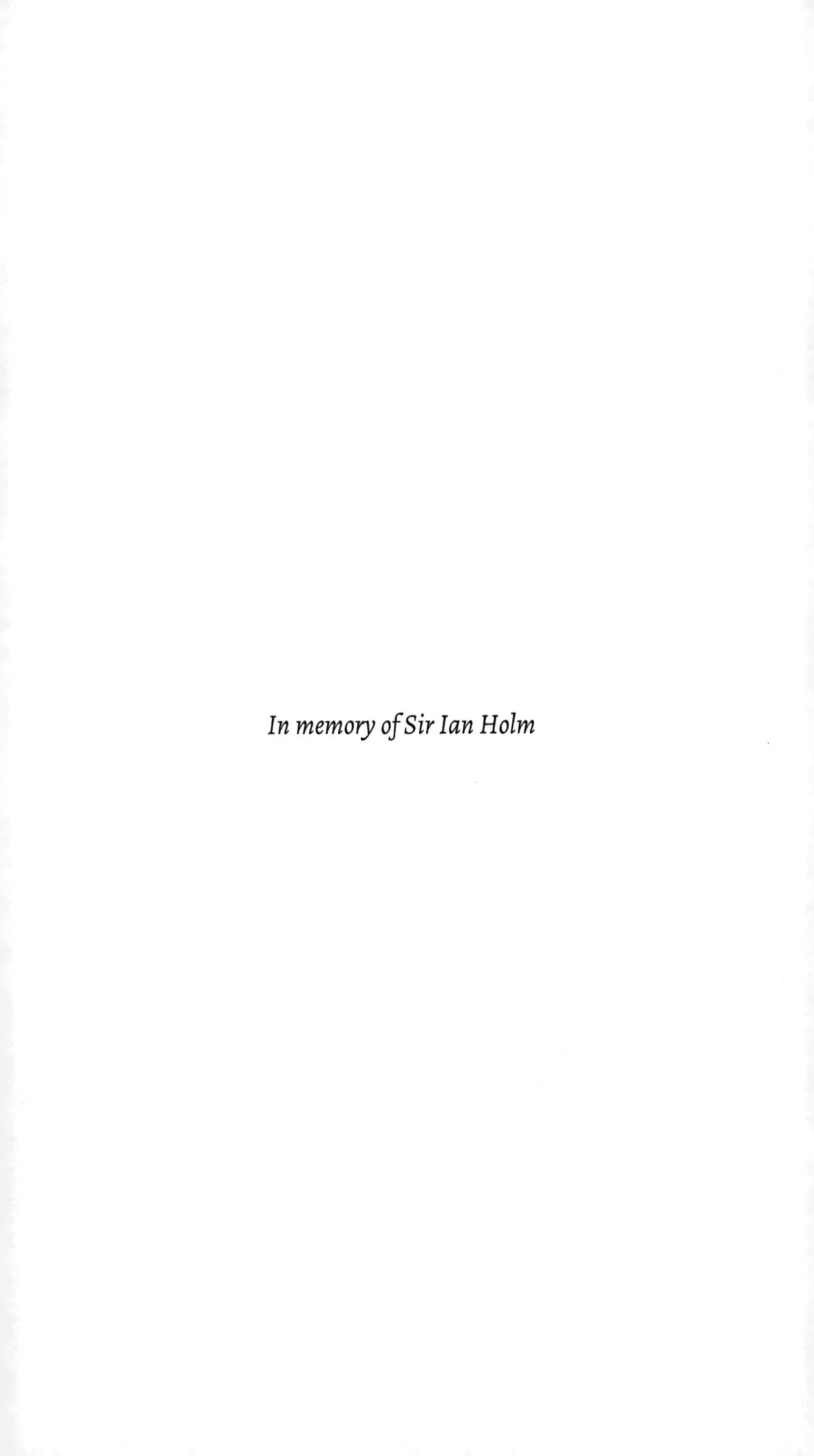

In memory of Sir Ian Holm

Midsummer Eve

Stephen Laws

"I do love you, you know."

"I know you do."

"Say my name. Say – 'I love you, Freya.'"

"I love you, Freya."

"Do you think it's a lovely name?"

"I do. I think it's a very lovely name."

"Why, thank you. That's a lovely thing to say. Are you comfortable?"

"Yes, thank you."

"It's just that you're a little tense. Do you want me to move a little bit?"

"Just a little bit. If that's okay?"

"Of course, it's okay."

"Maybe to your left a little. My hip's locking up a bit."

"To the left? Like this?"

"Yes... thank you. That's better."

"Good. This is lovely, isn't it? Just you and me."

"Yes."

"My parents didn't come from Scandinavia. Not from Denmark, or Norway or Sweden."

"No?"

"No, nor did my Grandparents on either side. Always North of England. Scotland maybe – way back. So maybe there's a connection back in the past somewhere. The Vikings used to raid the North of England a lot, some settled here. Lots of local words and dialect have 'Norse' roots. Did you know that?"

"No, I didn't know that."

"It's true. I asked my parents once if they'd called me 'Freya' because maybe there was some Scandinavian connection in the family. They said not. They just liked the name. Do you like the name?"

"Yes, I like your name."

"Do you really like it? Or do you *love* it?"

"Oh I *love* it, Freya."

"Oh, but you're *so* nice."

"Thank you."

"But I never quite believed them. Don't know why. I just didn't. I always felt there was something they weren't telling me. I just felt so *drawn* to Sweden, in particular. I know it sounds strange. But I felt, deep down, that there was *something*. If your parents are called Bill and Sandra, you just don't pick a name like 'Freya' for your daughter if it doesn't mean anything, do you?"

"Sounds like there must have been something."

"That's what *I* thought. And I just love Abba's songs. Do you like Abba?"

"Love them."

"So – the older I got and the more time that went by and various things happened, I just became besotted with Sweden and all things Swedish. Like there was something in my blood."

"Blood's thicker than water."

"How do you know? How can you say something like that?"

"Sorry. It's just what people say, isn't it...?"

"You've gone tense again. Are you all right? Are you comfortable?"

"Yes...yes..."

"'Are you sitting comfortably?' Hah! Do you remember that? Perhaps you're too young. They used to say that on the radio when I was little. 'Listen with Mother'. That's what it was called. This lady with a nice voice used to tell children's stories and there'd be lovely chimes and then her voice would say: 'Are you sitting comfortably? Then I'll begin...' And she would tell a story. I was very little then and it was a long time ago. Sometimes I think I must be very old. Do you think I'm old?"

"No, you're not old. You don't look old."

"How *do* I look?"

"You look lovely."

"Thank you. Are you sitting comfortably?"

"Yes."

"Then I'll begin. And I think I'll begin with Bjorn. That's a nice name, isn't it?"

"Yes, it is nice. A Swedish name."

"That's *right*. Oh, you're so sweet. And I think you really understand me. As well as loving me. You do love me very much, don't you?"

"Yes, Freya. I do love you very much."

"Mum and Dad bought me Bjorn when I was very young. I overheard them one night saying how worried they were about me, whether they shouldn't get some help, and maybe something like a little kitten might help me. It was all part of their trick, you see?"

"Trick?"

"Trying to pretend that they loved me when they didn't."

"Oh, I see."

"Do you? Do you really see? They said that they couldn't understand why I felt that they weren't my real Mum and Dad. But I knew. Deep down, I knew. The Swedish thing again, you see? Sometimes you just know. Deep inside, you *know*. They said the kitten would love me. Bjorn would really love me. (I gave him that name, of course.) But he didn't. He played and he ran about and he did all the things that little kittens do. But when I asked him to look me in the eyes to show that he loved me, he wouldn't do it. So I knew. I asked him lots of times, but he wouldn't do it. Or he'd do it, and look away at something else more interesting. So – you know – he had to be shown how mean he was to me. You're wriggling again."

"I'm sorry – it's just that I can't get... comfortable."

"Oh, I'm sorry. I'll move again a little. There. How's that? Does that feel better?"

"Yes, that's better. Thank you."

"Look me in the eyes. Tell me again how much you love me."

"I love you very much, Freya."

"That's a bit upside down but I know that you mean it. Not like Mum and Dad. Not like Bjorn. So one day, in the kitchen, Mum had a saucepan full of boiling water on the stove. The kitten was playing on the floor.

When Mum looked away, doing something else... well, that was that. She thought it was her fault. But you know, even when I was pretending to be upset and Mum was making all that awful noise, she still couldn't look me in the eyes and show me that she loved me. Even when Bjorn was buried in the garden, she – and Dad – pretended that they cared. You can still cry and look upset and kind and worried and caring – but not *really* care, deep down. I know that. I've seen that, felt it."

"You must have been very unhappy."

"Yes, I was. Yes. All I needed was the *proof*, you see? But how can you prove something that's not there?"

"You're a very caring person, Freya."

"I'm a very 'frayed' person. That's what my friend Jacqueline used to say. She used to say that underneath I was 'afraid' – like a scaredy cat. 'Fraid/Frayed', you see? And 'frayed', like something that's coming apart at the edges like a piece of cloth or rope or something. She said she could see I was mean and clever, once."

"You're not mean, Freya."

"No, I'm not. She was the one who was mean, saying those things. She didn't love me either, wouldn't look in my eyes. And then one day, we were sitting on that high wall – both together, facing the same way, both chewing on a piece of grass. And I said: "Jacqueline?" And she said: "What?" And I said: "Jacky leaned." Jacqueline. Jacky–leaned. You see? And she said: "What?" again. That's when I slapped my arm back against her chest and she went straight backwards off the wall. It was much, much higher on that other side. There was rubble down there, too; not grass, like on my side. Didn't mean for her to die. Just meant to teach her a lesson. Must have landed on her head. Fractured skull."

"Not your fault. Not if you didn't mean for her to die."

"You see? That's why I love you so much. You understand me so well."

"I do, Freya."

"What do you know about Midsummer's Eve?"

"Midsummer?"

"Midsummer's Eve."

"I don't think... I don't know. Why don't you tell me?"

"Say, 'Why don't you tell me, darling?'"

"Why don't you tell me, darling?"

"It's a big thing in Sweden. I've studied it a lot over the years, ever since I was a little girl. They have it all over the world, but it's much bigger and better in Sweden. Not like anywhere else in the world."

"It sounds lovely."

"It is, but it's more than that. It's a celebration of Summer, the Longest Day – like a little holiday where people light bonfires to ward off evil and witches and Bad Things. Some people say it's to celebrate the eve of the birthday of Saint John the Baptist, but I don't believe that bit at all. Do you believe in Christianity?"

"Do you want me to believe in Christianity?"

"Now what kind of question is that, silly? You either do or you don't."

"I'm... not sure."

"Well, it doesn't matter. The thing is – Midsummer's Eve's not about Christianity at all, I think. It's a time when two worlds come together for a little while. When things become...I can't think of a word. Can you think of a word?"

"No, Freya. I can't think of a right word."

"Do you want me to be cross?"

"No, darling! I really don't want you to be cross. It's just that – I don't know as much as you about Midsummer Eve. Please tell me more."

"Oh, I'm sorry. I'm like Little Miss Grumpy, aren't I? Well – it's celebrated all over the world. There's 'Beltane' – that's the Gaelic May Day Festival on 1st May. That's for Ireland and Scotland. And then in Denmark they've got 'Sankthans' – that's where they have the world's largest bonfire. Oh, it's all over the world really. But, like I said, I like what they do in Sweden best because, well you know, I feel as if that's where I really come from. They celebrate it so differently there, like there's magic in the air. Midsummer's Eve – on a Saturday between 19th June and 25th June."

"Like today?"

"Yes, darling! That's good. Like today. A very special day. Do you feel like it's a special day, today?"

"Yes, I do. Very special indeed."

"That's so good. You feeling that way, I mean. Midsummer Eve's like a... fertility rite, a celebration of Summer and good things. They eat and they drink and they dance. Do you know? It's the second most important national celebration in Sweden next to Christmas – and it's got nothing to do with Christian stuff, like I said. It's like a public holiday, really – Oh, it's wonderful. They have this thing called 'Sma Grodorda' where they dance around like little frogs. Little frogs! Can you imagine?"

"Yes, Freya."

"Makes me feel good just talking about it. All those happy faces. Never been there, you know. Sweden, I mean. But I've seen it on television. Laughing eyes. That's what they've got. Lots of laughter and love in their eyes."

"That's nice. That's lovely."

"Yes... it is. Not like my Mum and Dad's eyes."

"Their eyes? What about their eyes?"

"There was no love in them. All the time, when I was growing up and they kept telling me that they loved me, they really didn't love me at all. Not the way that I wanted to be loved. Not like the way you love me. Isn't that right?"

"I love you very, very much Freya."

"Oh – you're so, so sweet. But you see – they were very clever, my parents. Clever at pretending they loved me. My mother was particularly good at it, by making her eyes look as if they loved me. Not like my father. Know what I could see when I looked close into his eyes?"

"What could you see?"

"Fear."

"Not of you, surely. How could anyone be frightened of you?"

"There you go again, see? That's why I know you love me – because you just *understand* me so much. My father was frightened that I'd find out that his eyes were lying, and that I'd see the truth. See that he was only pretending that he loved me, and I'd find him out. Well

– it was just impossible, wasn't it? No one could bear to live with that kind of knowledge."

"Of course not."

"So there had to be a change."

"What kind of change, my darling?"

"Are you comfortable? You're wriggling again."

"It's my hip. The way we're lying here. It's cramping up."

"I'm sorry, my love. I'll move just a little bit more. How's that?"

"Better, thank you. You were saying?"

"Well, that's where the fire came in."

"The fire?"

"The house fire that killed my parents. Well, the fire finished the job, but they probably would have died anyway after I took their eyes."

"You... took their eyes?"

"Mum was first. She was very frail, and it wasn't hard to overpower her once I made my mind up on what had to be done. She was already in a wheelchair, so it didn't take much to wrap rope around her arms and get the gag in her mouth before she started making too much noise. Actually, the little bit of noise she made was quite helpful, really. Because Dad heard 'something' and came to investigate in the living room where we were – and I was waiting behind the door with a half plank of wood. Bonk! Down he went. Wrapped him up into a Midsummer's Eve parcel. Arms and legs, same as Mum. Then onto the sofa. Much easier than I thought. I'm very organised, you see. Always think and plan well ahead. Don't you think so?"

"Oh yes, Freya. You're very, very organised."

"The next part was the hardest."

"Can I have some water, Freya? I'm very dry."

"No. They wouldn't keep still, you see? Even though they were well tied up. Took one eye out of Mum and showed her what I'd always seen in it. The lie in it. Then showed Dad before I took one of his and showed Mum. They just refused to admit it. Made a lot of lying noise. But wouldn't admit about their lying eyes. Took Mum's other – left Dad with the one. Then I started the fire. Good job we lived out in the country, in that cottage. No one to see, no one to hear. Stood at the door and watched the fire take hold. Mum was already gone by then, I think, by the time the fire reached the sofa. Forgot to say – I left Dad with the one lying eye so he could see what was happening. I wanted to see, at the end, whether his defences would go down and he could see at last that I knew – *knew* – from the look in that one eye that he really didn't love me. But no. He kept the lie up right until the end when the fire took them both on the sofa and his last eye popped like a fried egg. Well – I ask you. What could I do? What could I say? Unacceptable, that's what it was. Completely unacceptable. I wouldn't even give them the pleasure of a response. I just turned my back on them and left. Can you blame me?"

"Not at all, Freya."

"Absolutely. I just threw those eyes over my shoulder, back into the room – back into the fire – and walked away. "

"I love you, Freya. I really do love you."

"Awww – you're so lovely. You say such nice things. And even though your eyes are upside down from where I am, I can tell that you're not lying to me. Don't you think it's funny?"

"Funny?"

"There's a 'y' in the middle of 'Freya' and a 'y' in the middle of 'eye' and a 'y' in the middle of 'lying'. But there's no 'y' in the word 'lie'. Funny, that."

"Yes, it is."

"There was an investigation, of course. But I just pretended to be in shock and because everything burned completely, there was no evidence to implicate me. I mean, the bodies and the eyes were all burned up so there was no evidence there, and I guess the ropes must have all burned up, too. The ropes were the only things that concerned me afterwards, but no – they never caused me a problem. Just all ash. Cottage had needed rewiring for years because Dad, the tight old scrote, wouldn't pay for it. We had sparks jumping out of the light sockets when you switched one on in the living room! So there were at least four or five places where the fire could have started, so I just said I was 'out for a long walk' and when I came back the place was like one of those big bonfires on Midsummer's Eve. Didn't have a mobile phone, did I? Wasn't allowed one. So I had to run to the village to raise the alarm. I should have got an Academy Award for that. So – justice was done. And I got a lot of sympathy, even from the police. Not love, of course. Just sympathy – which isn't the same thing, at all. No insurance for the house fire, either. Tight old scrote. Things got very different for me after that, on the money front."

"I'm so sorry to hear that, Freya."

"Thank you, my love."

"I wonder... do you think we can move somewhere else?"

"Why? Aren't you happy being here with me?"

"Oh yes, of course I am! Very happy. Very, very happy."

"And very much in love?"

"Of course! I love you very much, Freya."

"So why do you want to move, then?"

"It's just...well, this position is awkward. For both of us, I mean."

"I'm not complaining."

"And neither am I, Freya! Really...really, I'm not!"

"Love's not so straightforward sometimes. And sometimes, you have to suffer a little bit, just to get to the truth of whether two people love each other – or not."

"That's very true. Very, very true. Let's just stay where we are, then?"

"You see? It's when you say little things like that. Those little things that prove how much you love me. It was like that with George."

"George?"

"He's the reason I'm here. I nearly found true, true love with George. We just didn't have enough time together to prove our love for each other. So sad. But perhaps it was fate. Perhaps it was never meant to be. Poor George. Doesn't know what he's missing. You're wriggling again..."

"Sorry!"

"There, I've moved a little bit again. Is that better?"

"Yes, very much. Thank you."

"I think you mean – thank you 'darling?'"

"Of course I do. Thank you, darling. Thank you, Freya."

"Don't mention it. What's your name again?"

"Bryan. My name is Bryan."

"That's a nice name. Wait a moment! How do you spell your name?"

"B.R.Y.A.N."

"Oh, that's perfect! Don't you see, sweetheart? Not 'Brian' with an 'i' in the middle. But 'Bryan' with a 'y' in the middle! Just like 'Freya'! Just like we were made for each other. That's fate, isn't it? That's got to be fate."

"Yes, fate. Definitely fate."

"So – 'Bry-an': I was just telling you about George. That was two years ago. Just after Midsummer's Eve. I did what I was supposed to do. You know? The ritual?"

"No, I don't... The ritual?"

"Didn't I tell you? Silly me. Well – one of the special things about Midsummer's Eve, when two worlds come so close together, is the magic that can happen if you do things just right. The ritual, I mean. This is how it goes. On Midsummer's Eve, you jump over a fence *seven* times, and then pick *seven* different flowers. Then you put those seven different flowers under your pillow, and then you'll have a dream that will show you your future love. Well, I did just that on Midsummer's Eve two years ago. But here's the funny thing. I didn't have any dreams that night. Not one. Don't you think that's strange? I got up that morning, got changed, and had my oatmeal. *Waiting* for something. But no – nothing came. So I went for a walk. I was living in a Council house then, just off the High Street. There was hardly anyone about. But I could *feel* it. Feel that something was going to happen. And – what's your name, again?"

"Bryan."

"And Bryan – then the most wonderful thing happened. There was a car park, just next to this little supermarket. And there was one car parked there. Just the one. And in that car was a man, sitting there behind the wheel, reading a newspaper. I can't remember what the newspaper was, because when I got up close all I could see were his eyes. His beautiful blue eyes. And I knew then – just *knew* – that this was the something I'd been waiting for. That *he* was the person. He was the love I'd been waiting for, that I'd jumped the fences for, and that I'd put the flowers under the pillow for."

"So what did you do?"

"Well, I opened the passenger side door. He was very surprised. But that should have been my first clue that something wasn't quite right. Then he was angry, which was my second clue. That's when I jumped in and I just slammed that door and then he got really angry, demanding to know who I was and what did I think I was doing. So I had to show him the knife. Put it under his chin."

"And then what happened, Freya?"

"Well, he was frightened, of course. It was all so very sudden, you see? He started babbling then, which I didn't like very much. About how he didn't want any trouble, that he was just waiting for his wife to finish shopping in the supermarket before they went home. I listened for a while, hoping that he'd settle down and that the Midsummer magic would, well, work its magic. I thought that he just needed time. But he just kept getting more frightened, and I didn't like what I was seeing in his eyes. I certainly couldn't see the love that should have been there. When he said that I should just go and he wouldn't tell the police and that he just wanted to go home, that's when I really got cross with him. Losing all his dignity like that. So I told him to drive."

"Freya, please. It's hurting again."

"Sorry, love. There. That better?"

"Yes, thank you."

"So he drove. And I told him that he had a new home now. With me."

"But he wasn't the one, was he?"

"No, darling. He wasn't. I should have known from the beginning. I made him drive to my place. We went inside. I had to put the knife right across his throat to make him go through the front door, you know? Took him into his new home. Locked up – and waited for the magic to finally work. Waited for the love to turn up in his eyes."

"And did it?"

"No. But the police did. The next day. When his bitch wife came back to the car park and found him gone. I should have hidden the car. But I was too much in love, you see. Love can make you blind, can't it? They tracked the car from its licence plate. Broke into the house, eventually. It all got very nasty."

"I'm sorry."

"That's a very nice thing to say, but it wasn't your fault. So they took me away, and while they were 'assessing' me, it gave me time to think back to where I'd gone wrong. Like I said, I sort-of-knew I'd got it wrong from the beginning. The ritual, I mean."

"Seven fences, seven different flowers under the pillow."

"That's right, darling! Well remembered. So yes, there were seven different flowers under the pillow. But did the ritual need me to jump over seven *different* fences, or the *same* fence seven times? I jumped over seven different fences, you see? Goodness, I was worn out that day. And it didn't work. Which means, what I was supposed to do was jump over the *same* fence seven times. I had to wait a whole year for Midsummer's Eve again to get it right. Actually, it's been more than a year. When was I brought in here again? And don't forget to call me sweetheart when you answer me this time."

"A little more than a year-and-a-half, sweetheart."

"All that time in here. Waiting. So I planned it properly this time. Out in the prison exercise yard. With that lovely little miniature garden in the middle. Do they have miniature gardens like that in men's prisons?"

"I don't know, Freya. Sweetheart."

"Well it was like a magical sign when I saw it. With its cute little pretend fence all around. Been waiting for me all this time. Couldn't wait for today – Midsummer's Eve. This time I was going to get it right. And I did. Quickly. Before they stopped me."

"They thought you were just trampling the garden. Sweetheart."

"No! I was jumping over that same little fence seven times. And grabbing those little flowers. That was the risky part. Making sure I got seven different flower petals in my overall pockets before anyone tried to stop me."

"Freya, darling. Please. The knife. When you get – excited – telling the story. The point's right under my eye."

"I wish I could see your eyes the right way up, Bryan. They look as if they're full of love. But just to see them the right way up would be..."

"Well you can do that, darling! Really, you can. You can trust me. Because I really do love you. We could move from here, just a little."

"I suppose... I suppose it is a little uncomfortable. But let me finish. So the warders took me away and I spent last night here in 'solitary'. And it was glorious! All on my own, and when no one was looking I checked my overall pockets, praying that I hadn't lost the petals when they searched me for anything sharp. And, yes! There were *more* than seven different little petals in the lining of my pockets. I couldn't wait to put them under my pillow. And what a lovely night's sleep! There were no dreams again, like last time. But I wasn't disheartened. There was still time for the ritual to work, for the magic to happen. It just meant that I had to help it on a little."

"Which is why you pretended to have a fit in your cell this morning?"

"That's right, darling! You are so clever. That's when you and that female warder came."

"Janet."

"Yeah, her. I deliberately kicked my legs at her while I was on the floor. You know, like I was 'fitting'. So she would have to grab them. And then you..."

"Tried to hold your arms down."

"That's *right!* So I was able to get my arm around your neck and pull you down on top of me, backwards. Not very sexy, I know. I'd rather it was the other way around."

"But we can't stay like this, Freya. Let's just move around and..."

"It's not a real knife, you know."

"It *feels* like a real knife. And do you have to hold it *right* under my eye, like that? Sweetheart."

"It's a sliver of wood. Is that the right word, 'sliver'? Whatever. It's from a cupboard in the Rec Room. Managed to get it off and sneak it out simply ages ago. And the sharp end is from a razorblade. Not telling you where I got *that* from. But it took ages to fasten to the end."

"Maybe we could just get up off the floor, Freya – darling. I must be really heavy on top of you like this. The cell floor's very hard."

"It is – a little. But if the magic is going to happen, I don't want to spoil it."

"The magic *is* happening, Freya! It is! I love you very much."

"I knew it was you when you came through that door. But how can I be sure? I just can't see your eyes, properly, looking upside down like this."

"But you'll be able to see, right way up. If we just get to the bed."

"You are a *naughty* boy. Wanting to get me on the bed. But I'm not cheap, I'm not a slag you know. It has to be love, Bryan."

"Bryan, that's right! That's my name. With a 'Y'. And I do love you very much."

"I think they're getting ready to do something out there."

"No, Freya. They're not. They won't do anything. Let's you and I keep talking."

"I know they've wanted you to keep me talking while they work out what they're going to do. They've stopped whispering now."

"Really, Freya. I can feel the magic. It's happening right now. I can really feel it!"

"If only I could see your eyes the right way up."

"Just loosen your arm. Turn me around. I'll show you."

"I don't think there's time, Bryan."

"There is time, Freya. There *is*!"

"I can hear them. They're getting ready to come in. They're going to rush us."

"They're not. DON'T COME IN! Freya, let's..."

"Oh – sweet Midsummer's Eve – I've just thought of something I said earlier."

"Freya..."

"The truth was *there* all the time, darling. Looking me in the face. Eye to eye."

"Freya, tell me about the time when..."

"The ritual works. I know you're the one."

"Of course I am! Freya!"

"It's in all those old sayings, as well."

"I know, I know..."

"It's in the eyes."

"Sweetheart!"

"Love is in the eye of the beholder."

"Freya, please!"

"Oh my darling, you know what I have to do."

"Freya! Oh, my darling Freya. *Please...*"

"Love is blind..."

Midsummer Eve

C.C. Adams

"Everything changes once we identify with being the witness to the story, instead of the actor in it."

—Ram Dass

Streatham, South West London
27/03/08, 14:15

Gone.

The British Heart Foundation would be grateful. The fact that the bag and box of Rita's clothing he left outside the house yesterday had disappeared this morning was a good indication. Giving her clothes to friends wasn't an option: no one wanted to wear the garments of a dead woman. Especially not someone they knew.

Not something they wanted to be seen dead in.

He scoffed at the irony.

The path under his feet was firm and dry, not like the glistening of black tarmac yesterday morning after the rain. Not even seven o' clock and already the common twitched with early morning visitors: Lycra-clad joggers, earbuds in place. One shaggy German Shepherd trotting beside its mistress, off-leash. Beyond the tree line, the miniature figures of a football team in red-and-white kit, distant cries drifting back to Leonard, a backing track to the sound of his footsteps and the occasional roll of traffic from the main road.

Rita had loved all of this.

He had loved her.

He still did.

Twenty-seven years of marriage had seen their relationship pass through a variety of ups and downs like any couple, married or otherwise: from job promotion to job redundancy, from holidays in Europe to health scares. At sixty-eight, Rita was five years Leonard's junior, and less than three months after her birthday of friends and wine, Leonard's wife was dead. The two of them had been sat together in front of the TV watching *Strictly Come Dancing* and when Leonard quipped that he'd give Craig Revell something to smile about, Rita ignored him. It wasn't until, expecting at least some response (given that he had two left feet), he turned to his side and saw her slumped back against the sofa that he realised he had ignored *her*. His movement had then prompted more from her – and her body slid sideways down the sofa, head describing an arc and dragging silver-grey hair behind it. Shell-shocked, Leonard had called 999 and paramedics arrived soon after, pronouncing Rita dead at the scene. Cause of death? Pulmonary embolism.

Time slowed after that, as life carried Leonard along – since it had only stopped for his wife, not for him. Rita had already made provision in her will for both her family and her burial (as Leonard had). The couple never had any children or wanted any, so the lion's share of the will went to Rita's two younger brothers, and to Leonard himself.

Leonard slowed his pace, eyes fixed straight ahead. Looking but not seeing.

This close to the wood, you could smell the craftsmanship: rich. Sumptuous. Solid weight to the coffin as well, jolting his shoulder with each step they took. He'd grin and bear it, though. Rita spared no expense for her final send-off. Just what she deserved. He, of course, deserved to be at the front of the pallbearers, but that wasn't practical. As an old man, he was allowed the courtesy of helping to bear her coffin. The practical difficulty in lowering the coffin would be easier on him if he didn't have to take a corner of it. Human frailty aside, he'd played his part in escorting his wife. St. Leonard's Church was nearer – and smaller – but the grounds no longer took burials. So West Norwood Cemetery it was.

The sombre mood was maintained as they bore the coffin to its final resting place. Words were spoken in hushed tones. The coffin was covered over. Mourners spoke among themselves in stilted conversation – not in the mood to say much but feeling obliged to say something. Having already shed a few tears, Leonard eventually excused himself from the others and journeyed home to 'be alone with his thoughts'.

Some time later, the doorbell rang, as he expected it would.

Graeme. Also, as expected. Bald scalp gleaming, roll of flesh above the shirt collar. Between Graeme and Anthony, Graeme was the more altruistic of Rita's brothers. Of course, Leonard had invited him in – what else would he do? The two men made their way into the lounge; Leonard's gaze intent, and Graeme's gaze hesitant, hands clasped in his lap.

"Can I get you do something to drink? Tea? Coffee? Cider?"

Graeme barely bit back a smile. An inside joke – pear cider was Leonard's strongest indulgence, but Graeme was a whisky man. Drinks served, Leonard tapped the neck of a Kopparberg Pear on Graeme's glass of whisky with a soft clink, and both men sipped, blanketed in the quiet.

Graeme grew solemn. "How're you doing?"

It wasn't the time to be flippant. "I'm doing okay."

"You sure?"

"Well, it's not been easy," Leonard said, sitting back in his chair. "But dealing with so much of what comes next, it's kept me so busy. I've not had to spend so much time in my own head."

"Busy is good."

"That it is. That garden's been in need of a seeing-to for a while." Hopefully, Graeme couldn't see from this distance how much work it needed.

A slow nod. "Okay."

Silence.

"We just...we just want you to know that we're here for you."

"I know."

"And that you don't have to go through any of this alone."

"I know."

The rest of the conversation had been similarly forced, bordering on physically painful, because Leonard's shortcoming was *pride*. Graeme had even gone as far as to give him a leaflet for a nursing home. Not because Leonard couldn't fend for himself, but because he could use the companionship and social interaction that he wouldn't get from living alone. Perennial Estate. No reason it wouldn't be a real-life horror story like countless other nursing homes. Advancing years may have robbed him of physical strength, but *mental* strength? Oh, yes, he had that in spades. And the mind was like any muscle: exercise would make it fitter and stronger. But reading was a solo pursuit, as was chess, thanks to the ComputaChess set he had. Leonard knew he needed people more than ever now, but was afraid to admit it, especially after maintaining the façade for so bloody long.

Mind back in the present now, he slowed to a halt on the path. Up ahead in the distance, a Border Collie trotting ahead for a spell before slowing for its mistress to catch up. Leonard raised a hand and idly smoothed the wispy curtain of hair that wrapped around the back of his bald head. His hand rested there as he watched the animal.

What would I do with the damned thing? It would get tired of me too, I would imagine.

A dog was a poor substitute for a human, and while the dog couldn't articulate thoughts, the animal would no doubt pick up on the fact that the owner just wasn't happy – no matter how hard the dog tried. Misery all round.

Movement registered at the top of his periphery and by the time Leonard had processed it, the dog was already trotting up to his trouser leg, head down, sniffing him. The movement tickled the flesh of his leg, and he bent to pat the dog's head. "And who might you be? Hmmm?"

The dog looked up at him, eyes searching.

Misery all round.

Without warning, heat sprang to Leonard's eyes. The abruptness of it, the swell of grief choking him and he gasped, as the dog's owner closed the distance.

Turning on his heel, Leonard left the common the way he came, silently praying, *Please, don't follow me.*

He slammed the door behind him, barged into the lounge and eased his weight into an armchair. And shook his head in disgust – bloody hell: gone were the days when he could just *throw* his weight into an armchair. Now he *had* to do everything slowly.

He lifted a cool, wrinkled hand to his mouth and stifled a sob.

Tears slid free, burning beneath his eyelids and blurring his vision. Leonard sat that way for a while until the incessant tickling over his chin grew too much to bear and he had to resort to wiping his tears away on his sleeve. Minutes wore on and eventually the tears ran their course, turning to little more than thin crusted tracks on lined cheeks. Sobs dwindled to nothing; even the sense of wretchedness had faded, leaving behind little more than throbbing temples.

Cupping his elbows in his palms now, Leonard sat forward with a wan smile as a draught wafted into the room, gently easing the door ajar behind him. A truism of life: it didn't matter whether you were eight or eighty, everyone wanted to reach out and touch someone. If you were lucky, you found someone you could keep and hopefully they found the same in you. So, what happened when life came to an end for that person?

Chilly.

He couldn't be bothered to put the heating on.

Hours passed idly channel-surfing and watching TV had led him here. Cool sheets whispered beneath him as he slid into bed, still keeping to his side of the mattress. The fact that there was still a space behind him in bed didn't go unnoticed – how *could* it? – but at least he didn't cry in bed like he had done in the first few days

after she died.

She's not coming back either.

I love you, Rita.

And he did. But she wasn't coming back. All he had for comfort right now was the support of the bed and the quilting of the duvet. So, he pulled that up under his chin and lay there with his thoughts. Until growing fatigue eased them out of his grip and ushered him to sleep.

Had he known how much bloody hard work it would have been, Leonard wouldn't have bothered at all. Not that the weeds put up much of a fight, but the fact they were at ground level meant a lot of stooping and bending when he was in no fit state for either.

Bloody fool, you are.

And who else will do it? Won't do itself now.

A greying afternoon had Leonard working up a sweat like it was a midsummer evening, flannel shirt pasted to his back as he finished pulling up the last of the weeds. It wasn't like Graeme hadn't offered, but then, Leonard was used to suffering in silence. Plus, he needed all the exercise he could get: the use-it-or-lose-it mantra still holding firm. With difficulty; joints popping a chorus of cracked knuckles. The panel of freshly turned black earth in front of him looked like a...

like a grave.

Maybe I shouldn't have.

Sure, the garden had given him something to do – but apart from the fact that it involved a *garden,* Leonard knew precious little about gardening. Had he said as much to Graeme, the other man would have insisted on coming around to help, or at least supervise. And Leonard didn't want either of those things. After all, he was old. Not stupid.

Some might think the two would—

Behind him at the top of the garden path, the kitchen door opened.

With the slowness of the curious, Leonard turned to look over his shoulder. The kitchen door hung open, motionless.

Mouth agape, he narrowed his gaze at the door. Nothing but the occasional roll of traffic from the main road, and the sound of a TV from one of the neighbours' houses.

Hmmmm.

Leonard made his way to the top of the path, pulling off his gardening gloves as he did so. Any time he or Rita went out into the garden, they always pulled the door in behind them: what you didn't want was a strong wind that would slam the door shut and break the glass. The door was light, but it was a newer construction: sturdier. Meaning that it would stay shut unless someone opened it.

He rested his hand against the edge of the door, and it wavered in his grip. The lock and handle looked fine, more or less as good as the day it was first installed. Somewhere above him, inside the house, the bedroom door closed.

Fingers, gripping the door harder now.

Sure, the air was chilly, but there wasn't a wind blowing now, not even a breeze – and if there wasn't a breeze *outside* the house, there wouldn't be one *inside* the house either.

Pulling the door in behind him, he made his way upstairs, proceeding on the balls of his feet with each step until he reached the landing. His bedroom door hung open.

A wave of goose bumps crept across his shoulders and he gave a shudder. He peered around the door, seeing the bed: made, the dresser: tidy, his robe over the back of the chair: just as he'd left it. Everything... just as he'd left it.

Except the door. And how would the door be open if he heard it shut?

It didn't slam shut to spring back open with force, so that meant—

You stop that.

THAT meant someone opened it.

There's no one here but you.

Leonard scanned the room again, his gaze searching the furthest corners of skirting board to the corners of the ceiling. Searching the remaining rooms of the house did indeed confirm that there was no one else there but him. So, he returned to the lounge and seated himself with a cup of tea, with the same wordless mantra running through his head. Mental images of assorted sensory input: the reassurance of a soft warm hand, made frail over the passage of years; frail, but no less affectionate. Floral scents that clung to the hollow above the collarbone. A brush of lips against the earlobe when wisecracks were whispered.

There's no one here but you.

He scoffed, the sound scraping the silence.

Across the room, pictures ignored him from the mantelpiece. Him and Rita, in several pictures that would pass for snapshots of well-rounded life in the golden years. A photo of them walking barefoot in wet sand along the shoreline of a beach. Cornwall or somewhere? All he could remember was some young girl breaking company from her boyfriend, asking if they wanted a picture taken. Turned out it had been a pretty good call. Another couple of pictures: both taken by the same photographer. One of them with Rita looking over his shoulder as she hugged him from behind, the other picture of her clasping his face and kissing his cheek so hard, the smacker nearly left his ears ringing.

Leonard pushed to his feet and picked one of the pictures off the mantelpiece. Pressure bore down on his shoulders and he sighed as he threw his head back.

At least you were active, and you stay active. That's you living a full and happy life now, isn't it?

Mens sana in corpore sano?

There's no one here but you.

Wasn't *that* the truth?

The pressure on his shoulders increased.

Easing his shoulder back as though elbowing someone away tilted the picture he held in his hand, the glass now catching the light at a different angle.

But not enough to obscure the pale and eyeless face glaring at him from behind.

Horrified, Leonard spun, dropping the picture in the process – and in a whirl of motion, caught a blurred impression of an ashen silhouette. Somewhere out of his field of vision, a *flumpf!* as the picture hit the carpet.

His breath, coming in short, shallow gasps.

The room stood silent, daring him to move.

Fingers groping behind him, Leonard found the corner of the table and gently eased his weight onto it, hearing it creak in response. That was some reassurance – because if he didn't hold onto the thing, he was pretty sure he would pass out.

He rolled his shoulder back, feeling none of the pressure or discomfort from earlier.

Hands on me?

Oh, God.

There's no one here

no one you can see, at least—

Shut up!

He licked his lips, mouth open in a frown of worry. Mental tirades never came with an off-switch, and if they did, the thing would never bloody work.

Senses taut, he bent and retrieved the picture, holding it face down, refusing to look at it, and repositioned it on the mantelpiece as though he himself was made of glass – a brittle and delicate thing.

The room was still empty.

There were things that, with the passing of years, grew easier to accept than others. Greying of hair and its subsequent loss. Progressively less physical strength, where even something as simple as taking a flight of stairs became a workout. Deteriorating eyesight. Loss of libido...and bladder control. Those were things that Leonard conceded would fail, but he'd be damned if he didn't preserve what little he had. That applied to mental assets as well as the physical ones – in short, he wasn't crazy.

He wasn't hallucinating either.

But what he had seen was impossible.

A chill afternoon brought a clear night to Streatham. Wind blew grease-spotted wrappers of eaten fries along pavements. Traffic lights continued their three-colour ritual for progressively less traffic. Away from the thump of loud music inside late-night bars, and rats sniffing out scraps in dark corners, residential back streets sat silent: lines of terraced houses with windows fronting dark rooms.

In one such house, the temperature fell, like a feather gently brought to land. Cold air settling in the hallway.

Along the staircase and the landings.

Throughout the bedrooms.

Unseeing, Leonard's eyes moved beneath their lids, the bridge of his nose creasing for a moment.

And still, temperature in the room fell.

Enough to buoy Leonard from the depths of sleep to the surface of consciousness.

There in the darkness, his eyelids fluttered, presenting nothing but a haze through the veil of his eyelashes.

And a pale silhouette.

As his eyes adjusted to the gloom, so did his mind.

The silhouette hung there. Eyeless.

Watching him.

Leonard stared, eyes widening in horror.

One pale figure, ashen in appearance like when he had first seen it reflected in the picture. Gaunt. Blank eyeholes in a long angular face, atop a slim body.

His fingers groping for a fistful of duvet, Leonard drew it up under his chin. The figure made no effort to move; it simply hung there, watching.

Leonard's pulse began to pound in his ears. Not wanting to make any sudden moves, it didn't take long before his muscles and joints protested in discomfort. The figure had no eyes, but from the expression on the face, it held him in nothing but cold contempt. Glaring at him.

Some time later the figure dissolved into the air, as

insubstantial as cigarette smoke. And that, somehow, was more terrifying, because Leonard didn't doubt for a minute that the figure – unseen as it was now – hadn't gone for good.

Far from it.

Graeme thanked the gardener and showed him the way out before returning to join Leonard in the dining room. He found Leonard standing by the window, looking at the garden.

"Not a bad job, eh?"

No answer.

Graeme took a seat, hitching up the legs of his trousers as he did so. "And all you need to do is water and weed it once in a while. You can use the Flymo as well."

"Yes."

Graeme brought his hands together in a hollow clap. "I don't know about you, but I'm parched. Can I get a drink of water?"

"Of course."

Leonard made his way into the kitchen and returned with two glasses of water, holding one and leaving the other on the table.

"Hey – why don't you sit down?"

Leonard looked back at Graeme over his shoulder and in that instant, Graeme saw something birdlike: the way the head bobbed like that of a vulture. Right down to the curious gaze and hawkish nose. The curtain of hair wrapped around the back of his shining scalp. The old boy didn't miss a trick. When Leonard took his seat, he took it with deliberation, and took a swig of water before returning the glass to the table.

"Graeme," he said at last, "how long have you known me?"

Graeme gave a whispery laugh of surprise. As far as openers went, this sounded ominous already. "How long? As long as you and Rita were married – before that, even. The better part of thirty years, and some change."

"And how well do you think you know me?"

Graeme narrowed his gaze at him. The old man sat with his hands on his knees and sat straight – in spite of the fact that he had no such training, Leonard held himself with military bearing. Proud. Alert. "I'd say I know you pretty well. Leonard...where are you going with this?"

Leonard exhaled sharply through his nostrils, his mouth drawing into a tight line as he did so. Finer creases appeared. "I hope that's true, because I'm going to tell you something that might have you question me. Let me reassure you that I'm not a senile old man, despite what I'm about to tell you."

"And that would be...?"

Leonard's chest heaved. "I think there's a ghost in this house."

Graeme's mouth fell open as he searched the old man's face, waiting for the punchline.

None came.

"You think...that there's a ghost in the house?"

A terse nod.

"What makes you think that?"

Leonard leaned in closer, and behind the old man's glasses, his gaze steeled on Graeme. "Because I've *seen* it."

"Oh."

Of all the things that Leonard could have told him, that would never have featured anywhere on the list. And he knew Leonard well enough. Those thankfully rare occurrences when Rita was sick, the first point of contact was understandably her husband: the man who prided himself on common sense and pragmatism. Of course, no man would cheat the reaper and time would win out sooner or later: that was just the nature of things. The years would weaken the muscles, dampen the hearing, dull the senses, blur the memory and mental acuity – all part of the ageing process. At seventy-three, Leonard was an old man, but didn't look like a crazy one.

What did a crazy man look like? Maybe someone with a wealth of conviction.

"So, you saw a ghost."

Leonard gave a humourless smile.

"What are you going to do about it?"

"That's what I'm asking you."

Graeme flinched as though he'd been slapped in the face. "What?"

"What can I do about it?"

That brought him up short. The fact that Leonard had patiently led up to this didn't help any – nothing could have prepared him for it. What to do about a ghost in the house? Graeme was still trying to process the idea that there *was* a ghost in the house. His mind fought for traction on a slick surface of reason. If he didn't give honest advice to this effect, Leonard would know Graeme didn't trust him. Which was partly true, but still...

"Leonard...you'll understand this is a lot to take on faith now."

"So, you don't believe me?"

Now it was Graeme's turn to offer a smile lacking humour. "I'd be pretty naïve to take it on face value, especially without evidence. I know you to be a reasonable man, and that's partly what worries me. No, I don't think you're crazy – or senile. Outside of what I think about...ghosts, I'm not sure I'd want to stick around here long enough to actually meet one."

"So, what would you suggest I do?"

Graeme opened his mouth to protest, but Leonard laid a forestalling hand on his knee, the grip warm and firm through his trouser leg.

"Just proceed as though you lived alone. With a ghost. What would you do?"

"Leonard..."

The grip tightened. "Humour me."

"I suppose...I suppose I'd try to get rid of it."

"How?"

Graeme's mouth fell open in silent exasperation: *really?*

"I suppose...I don't know. Ask it to leave, maybe? If there's a ghost here, maybe it's got a reason for being here. Maybe it's a sense of something familiar, or a message it needs to pass on to a loved one, or something it wants before it can leave? It could be anything."

Silence hung between them. Through the lenses of his glasses, Leonard was stern and resolute; Graeme's face, usually cheerful, now pained with a predicament as difficult as it was unexpected.

"Leonard," Graeme began, eyes downcast for a moment. "I want you to hear me out now. Or, at least, humour me."

"Must I?"

"Yes – you must." And although there was no smile on Graeme's lips, the creases at the corners of his eyes said otherwise. "This is a lot to take on face value. That's not to rule out your story completely, but these aren't the most ideal circumstances for you. The loss of a loved one – *our* loved one too, mind you – adapting to a new routine. Maybe other challenges besides. Ghost or not, we accept this can be a trying time for you.

"And I know..." At this point, Graeme hung his head before pressing on. "Look. I know this came up before, but Perennial—"

"Graeme." Glaring at the younger man, Leonard tapped his finger on Graeme's chest. "I'm *old*. Not *senile*. So understand the difference, yes?"

Cheeks flushed, and Graeme's jaw worked. "I understand that. But beyond the difference, here's something you need to understand regardless. Corny as it might sound, you don't get out much. You socialise even less. What Perennial Estate may give you is a sense of community. Belonging."

"I belong *here*."

"From what you've told me, so does something else."

Clapping a stern hand to his mouth, Leonard

exhaled through his nose. Arguing with somebody was easy. Regardless of whether you won the argument or not, you were still arguing with a human being, someone with a human sensibility. A ghost wasn't human, so couldn't be expected to have the same sensibility. Reasoning with one – assuming it was possible – wouldn't be easy. "So, what are you saying?"

"The same as before. We're here for you. That we don't want you to go through this alone."

Leonard sat silent for a while, a wistful smile in place, and then spoke at last. "There's just one other thing."

"What's that?"

"You mentioned that if I wanted to get rid of the ghost, I could try asking it to leave."

"Yeah."

"Well..." Leonard's chest heaved. "What if it doesn't want to?"

Stupid question.

That's what it was: a stupid question.

Because he'd articulated his fear, he'd now breathed life into it.

Did he really expect Graeme to believe him? Part of him did – but what did he *really* expect? Would he have acted any differently if their roles were reversed? Probably not.

Now he lay there in bed, duvet drawn up under his chin. The bedside lamp switched on, bathing the little table in a spotlight of sickly yellow. Throwing dark shadows across the rest of the room in the process. Fatigue wore heavily on him, but he would fight it. Those fears, seemingly trivial in the light of day and company of others, weren't easily dismissed in the dead of night.

He scoffed to himself.

Another mental tirade, playing across his mind in Rita's voice. *Silly old fool, you'll make yourself sick with worry, won't you? Why don't you just turn out the light and get some bloody sleep? You'll have to sleep sooner or later.*

That brought him no comfort. For all the sensory recollection, the tone and flow of her voice, the floral scent of her, he felt more alone than ever. Because the memory was here, but *she* wasn't.

Leonard sniffed in disdain, a pang of sadness washing over him. He clutched the duvet tighter, feeling fabric slide across his knuckles. He couldn't hang onto the duvet forever. Sooner or later he'd tire, his grip would give out, fatigue and stress would wear him out to the—

Wait a minute.

Wait.

Casting a sidelong glance at the room, Leonard inhaled slowly, deeply.

A floral scent hung in the air. Not that he could pinpoint where exactly it came from, but it was *there*. As was a chill in the room.

Beyond the bedroom, the door to the adjacent room opened. Whispering of wood across carpet as the door to Leonard's bedroom eased open.

Leonard lay stiff in bed, wide-eyed.

Trembling.

No air blew through the house; no visible guest or intruder entered the room, no sound of footsteps. But the door hung open, where it was clearly shut moments ago.

Leonard swallowed.

And this was the quandary, because what he wanted to do right now was run. Arthritis and infirmity be damned, he would pick himself up if only he could muster the courage and throw himself down the bloody stairs if he could.

Something buzzed beside him and he turned with enough force to bounce the bed, creaking the springs in the process. The light bulb in the bedside lamp, brighter as it buzzed

Nonononononono...

and dimmed, deepening shadows across the room, blurring outlines.

Pleeeeease...

The bulb, buzzing like a dying insect, and there was nothing he could do about it. Certainly not change the bulb or get out of bed to flick on the overhead light. No. *That* would involve moving in the dark. There and then, Leonard would have had as much chance as moving the house itself.

Light from the bulb dimmed to the glowing line of the filament, disappearing with a *pfffpt*, plunging the room into darkness.

No, please, no...

He didn't dare close his eyes now.

He didn't dare move either.

Moments crawled by, bringing clarity to the gloom as they did so. Those shapes obscured in darkness subtly revealed themselves: the edge of the bed, the outline of the dresser, the edge of the radiator beneath the window. Leonard's senses strained at their boundaries on high alert. His pulse still racing.

The apparition hovering at the foot of the bed.

With a gasp, Leonard shrank back against the mattress.

If the apparition had seen this, it gave no indication. Crowned by a hazy impression of lank hair, the eyeless face stared straight ahead, the arms hung by its sides. It didn't move.

Leonard chewed his lip, and inhaled—

The eyeless face turned to him. But that floral scent hung in the air, thicker now.

The apparition drifted closer around the bed, outlines of the room visible through the haze of its form. It bent over Leonard and he looked into its face. Through it, through twin holes of darkness at the ceiling above and behind it.

Trembling.

Hazy as it was, being so close to the figure picked out subtleties in its appearance: hollows where cheeks would be, lines near the eyes where you'd...you'd expect wrinkles, creases...yes, creases around where the lips would be.

Leonard swallowed. Mouth dry of saliva, a click sounded in his throat and he gasped in panic. The word tumbled out.

"R-Rita?"

The ghostly face drew back, weighing him.

Bad enough that Leonard had tried to speak, and that had taken what little courage and resolve he already had. No way could he bring himself to talk—

The figure dissolved into the darkness.

Leaving Leonard to stare at the empty space.

You should have asked it to leave.

It. Her.

As easy as that, is it?

Steam curled off the surface of the tea, and Leonard watched it rise. He couldn't drink the tea like that, but right now, he needed to feel something real and mundane. Plus, it was hot enough to burn him silly. Even picking it up would have been something of a mission. So he held the cup on the table in both hands, where it trembled in his fingers.

Maybe it's got a reason for being here. Maybe it's a sense of something familiar, or a message it needs to pass on to a loved one, or something it wants before it can leave? It could be anything.

Not now, it couldn't.

What little sleep Leonard had managed was broken and shallow. At some point in the night, he had mercifully passed out from fear. Woken during the dawn to find the mattress damp beneath him, and the smell of fish around him.

Of course, bedwetting was now the least of his worries.

Unable to sleep, he decided he would make himself

some tea and survey the rest of the house. Signs of a strong wind having blown through the other rooms were evident, from the extra length of toilet paper hanging from the roll to the scattering of opened mail from the corner of the lounge table. What the wind couldn't explain was why pictures were blown from the mantelpiece, but the glass from the frames were cracked as though they had been hit with a hammer. Hard enough to scratch the photograph inside.

Those pictures he had now put back on the mantelpiece with trembling hands, expecting that an unseen rebuke would come at any moment. For now, the pictures sat where they were before, cracks spider-webbing and obscuring the photos inside.

Maybe it's a sense of something familiar, or a message it needs to pass on to a loved one, or something it wants or... or...

He and five others, black-suited, bore the ungainly weight of her coffin.

Him bearing emotional weight, boxing the last of her cashmere.

Maybe it's a sense of something familiar...

In terms of familiarity, he wasn't sure on that one. Assuming he was right in who or what was visiting him, he didn't pick up on that right away. From a memory of Rita's lined face, resting on his shoulder and smiling up at him, to the apparition watching him in the middle of the night? No similarity he could see. What did that leave? A message?

Which is...?

Leonard sat back in his chair and pinched the bridge of his nose. If there was a message, what was it? His head throbbing from both anxiety and lack of restful sleep made it hard to focus.

Maybe it's you.

Me.

How can you see her? Because she can see you?

Perhaps because you're closer to her now.

Closer to death.

His breath hitched.

As a couple who lived together for years, there was little they didn't share or communicate. Neither was married before, and both had made the commitment that they would say 'I love you' every day, hold hands and kiss every day – the seemingly small gestures that would build a strong foundation over time. God forbid that if one were annoyed at the other, they would talk about it and resolve their differences, or at least compromise. Such efforts were the bedrock of a strong relationship.

Which is...?

But the embolism had robbed them of that.

Leonard cradled the cup in his hand, thoughtfully looking at his tea.

Perhaps because you're closer to her now.

"Huh." Pensive now.

Having lived a full life, death didn't scare him nearly as much as that revelation.

Maybe one last gesture was all it took.

He gave a chuckle, which came out forced. Shaky.

❖

Light glinted along the length of the arrow on the pen's cap. Leonard rolled the pen between forefinger and thumb. Parker. As solid now as they were back then. Truth told, he was surprised the damn thing could still write – it had been that long since he last used it. The need for cheques had grown less frequent, as had the compulsion for crossword puzzles.

Pen still in hand, he tore away the top sheet of the pad, scowling when the head of the page ripped. Yanking away the sheet, the rest of it came away cleanly, leaving a notch torn in the middle of the page. Still, it didn't matter too much. What was more important was that he could read what was written.

Oh, God.

Reading it: the least of his worries.

Sage. Sage is for... sage is for...

He shook his head, sighing in frustration. This was where grief and loss led the old: loneliness and bedwetting.

You had an excuse.

Really? No one else will see it like that.

No one else knows what you're going through

– and isn't that always the way?

The day had drifted quietly and uneventfully, as had Leonard himself. He hadn't ventured outside (which had surprised him, given the circumstances), but he'd seen enough to know the day outside was grey with a white gold sun tingeing the edge of the clouds it hid behind. And, of course, the sun would eventually sink into evening. Shadows slowly mustered their courage and crept from dark corners, growing larger in silence as the evening wore on. He sat on the bed, weighing the pad in his hand.

No time like the present, eh? The present's a gift. Valuable.

Goose bumps broke across his shoulders and he shivered.

Valuable, yes?

He'd since changed the bulb in his beside lamp, only for the bulb to appear as dead as the one that died the previous night. Similarly, on checking all the lights in the house, all of those were dead. Checking the main panel behind the cupboard door in the hallway told him what he already knew: electricity still served the property, the fuses all in place and unscathed. Which *again* told him what he already knew: the problem lay elsewhere. Presenting him with a silent house through the course of the day did nothing to convince him he was *alone* in that house. Muted conversations that came through the walls from the neighbours offered a scrap of comfort, but nothing more.

His gaze fell to the page.

"H-hello, love." He swallowed. God, his voice sounded so *fragile*. Thumb caressing the pad, he pressed on. "This is strange for me. Maybe it's...strange for you too."

Around him, the room sat quietly. Furniture. Shoes resting under the bed: only *his* shoes now. His coat, hanging on the coat hook on the back of the bedroom door.

"I'm sorry if this is strange for you." He hung his head. Closed his eyes as he fought to keep his thoughts in order. Tears fattened beneath their lids, and the first tear slid free down his cheek, joined by its neighbours. It hit the pad with a *plop,* soaking a circle into the page. "I wish we would have" – and here, his voice cracked – "had more time. But I guess..."

Perhaps because you're closer to her now.

He looked at the page. Beyond the blur of tears and the task at hand, he couldn't read what was there, much less remember it. Somewhere downstairs, a door opened.

Go... go on.

"...we don't."

Silence.

Something came to rest on his shoulder and he jumped, turning toward the source of the pressure. There was nothing there, but the pressure remained: a firm and invisible weight on his shoulder. Leonard pushed to get to his feet and the force magnified instantly, rooting him in place.

Whimpering, his hold on the pad weakened, where it slid from his lap and hit the floor in a flurry of pages.

"I... I..."

come on, think, please – think...

"I love you. But maybe we need to...move on." The last word was almost a question.

Glass cracked behind him, and his head whipped around to it. One section of the window now boasted a diagonal crack. As he watched, cracks shot through another two sections of window.

Panic forced him forward and he wrestled from under the unseen grip. Something held fast on his shirt, firm enough to rip the stitching as he tore free.

Stumbling from the room, the door swung open hard behind him: wood splintered. As Leonard stumbled from the room and rounded the banister, his foot slipped over the edge of the top riser. Throwing his hand back, he barely broke his fall as he clutched the banister post. Momentum pulled his grip free and he slid downstairs in a flurry of limbs, landing at the bottom in an ungainly heap. Pain flared in his hip.

Hauling himself to his feet, Leonard stumbled to the front door.

Glass in the door's windows fractured: one section at a time.

Oh, no, oh, God, no.

Staying in the house wouldn't help him. So where would he go?

Yanking at the door now, with nothing to show for it but a rattling of the lock. Scared beyond coherent thought to reason that the knob needed turning before opening the door.

"Nononono ... nonono..."

Fingers smooth with desperation, they at last slid away from the knob, Leonard in turn sliding down the wall, wide-eyed.

Weeping in fear.

His breath coming in short, shallow gasps.

Please let me out of here. Somewhere, anywhere, Perennial Estate – just let me out of here.

They'll think you're a crazy old man.

I don't care! I don't!

Don't you? Liar!

Please, please, please...

Midsummer Eve

Kelly White

Blurred shadows ripple through the video. A flash of white-yellow glare from the sun fills the screen before the camera shifts focus and the shadows coalesce into branches. They drift in a breeze, waving at the summer blue sky. The low shush of the wind is audible in the microphone. There is a rush of bark and leaves as the camera pans to a dirt path that threads through the trees.

A woman is limping along the path, moving away from the camera. The screen shakes with the rhythm of someone walking as the camera moves forward. Heavy breathing is audible over the shuffle of footsteps. The woman stops and tilts her head, listening. The camera jerks left and the screen is partially obscured by a tree as the woman turns to look over her shoulder.

The camera zooms in on the woman's face, hovers unsteadily on her bloodshot eyes and puffy cheeks until she turns away. It pans down over muddy, grass-stained jeans, pans up. Her t-shirt is ripped. It lingers on her exposed bra strap and the angry red scratches that run the width of her back, then zooms out again.

The woman leans against a tree, brushes hair from her eyes and rubs a hand over her face. She is talking to herself, trying not to cry. The movement of her lips is visible but her voice is faint, barely a murmur. She grips something in one hand. The pocket knife glints as it catches the sun. She scans the trees, looks back the way she came. The camera snaps down to show the ground, the edge of a boot. A horn sounds, exploding through the audio.

Chrissy shuffled her shoulders away from the stickiness of the seat. The car was uncomfortably warm, even with the rush of thick motorway air through the vents. The sun was slipping across the sky, the glare from the road and the cars in front threatening to blind her. She could barely see the Sat Nav, or hear it over Paul's CD.

Paul and Lydia were in the back seat, his eyes half closed, head nodding to the bass from the speakers, a half empty alcopop bottle balanced in his lap. Lydia rested her head against his shoulder and he turned to bury his face in her long hair. She held up her phone, grinning, and took their selfie.

Matt was in the passenger seat, hunched over a book the size of a brick, his long legs folded into the footwell like a piece of human origami. He had always been that way, able to read anywhere under any circumstances.

The track on the CD ended, and as the first notes of the next song drifted out of the speakers Paul whooped right in Chrissy's ear. "Turn it up, Chris."

Chrissy felt the thud of the bottle against the floor behind her and rolled her eyes. Lydia squealed and shuffled across the back seat.

"Shit." Paul scrambled for the bottle and Chrissy felt the impact of his head through the back of her seat. It had been like this all the way from London. Matt glanced over and they shared a brief look of understanding. Then Paul's warm hand was on her shoulder.

"Sorry, Chris. I, erm..."

"Don't worry about it. Next stretch of hard shoulder, I'll just stop and chuck you out." She met his eyes in the rear-view mirror.

There was a flash of panic on his face in the second before she smiled and stuck her tongue out at him. Matt held his hand out for a high five without looking up from his book. Chrissy slapped his hand, then reached to turn the music down. She was developing a headache that felt like grit behind her eyes. Paul laughed and ran a hand through his hair.

"Seriously, don't worry about it." She smiled. Paul disappeared behind the seat and reappeared with a fresh bottle. He held it out for her. "Driving."

"Shit. Yeah, sorry." He leant back in his seat and took a swig, then held it out for Lydia. She reached for the bottle and then squealed again.

"We're here. It's this exit, right?"

Paul leant forward between the front seats. "Chris, it's this one. Take this exit. We're here." Chrissy read the gantry sign – Junction 6, Birmingham, NEC and Airport.

Lydia held up her phone. "Everybody smile. Folk festival road trip."

"Just a second, Lyds." Chrissy indicated and moved onto the slip road. She glanced at the Sat Nav, the thin trees that lined the edge of the road casting just enough shadow for her to make out the display. "Sat Nav says another fifteen, twenty minutes."

"Yeah, but nearly." Lydia leant forward and snapped a photo of the side of Chrissy's face. She looked at her phone screen and made a chef's kiss gesture. "Perfect."

Chrissy shook her head and smiled. She took the third exit towards Coventry and Stonebridge Island. How was somewhere this close to Birmingham Airport going to feel authentic? Her vote had been for Stonehenge.

The thick scrub of grass drying at the sides of the motorway had been replaced with looming trees, their bark cracked with age and their branches swollen with leaves. The edges of the narrow tarmac road were crumbling into the dirt. Chrissy slowed the car. The sun reached through the canopy, grasping at the car with impatient fingers.

They peered through rolled down windows, trying to see beyond the trees. The mechanical rumble of the engine felt intrusive in the unexpected slice of countryside. Lydia held her arm out of the window, allowing the cooler air to flow over her bare skin. Paul turned from the window and took another swig of his drink.

"This is going to be epic. A proper old-school folk festival."

Matt forced his book into the glove compartment and turned in his seat. "Do you actually know anything about this thing, other than where it is?"

Paul gestured with the bottle in his hand. "Something about an ancient tradition. The power of the sun. And trees."

"Trees?"

"An oak tree, I think. Look, the dude on the internet promised a party."

"You said you got the tickets off a website," Chrissy said.

"Yeah. Well, not exactly. It was a forum actually. You know, like a chat room. I haven't got physical tickets, but our names are most definitely on the guest list."

"Right." Chrissy took a deep breath. She eyed the Sat Nav. According to the display they were only a few minutes out, but the blue loading circle was flickering up intermittently. It kept dropping the signal.

"You realise how sketchy that sounds?" Matt asked.

"Relax will you." Paul exaggerated a sigh. He fidgeted in his seat and pulled a pocket knife from the back pocket of his jeans. He held it up as if he was performing a magic trick and flicked the blade free. "Anything happens – and it won't – I got you covered."

Lydia looked at the knife and giggled. "Why would you need that?"

"For fuck's sake." Chrissy tightened her grip on the steering wheel.

The wooden gate was decorated with foliage. Thin branches bloated with leaves had been woven around the slats. Clusters of yellow, star-shaped flowers trailed through them, tied in with red and orange and yellow ribbons, like a rustic dreamcatcher. An unpleasant musk drifted through the windows as Chrissy manoeuvred the car through the gate and onto a dirt track. Matt leaned out the window and plucked a stem of the yellow flowers as they passed, ignoring Lydia's show of wrinkling her nose.

A mechanical purr drifted through the trees ahead, followed by the rush of escaping air and the tinny sound of fairground jingles played through worn-out speakers. The dirt track opened out onto a grassy field bathed in sunlight. It flooded the car and Chrissy raised a hand to shield her face. As her eyes adjusted, she saw the gnarled silhouette of a tree erupting from the middle of the field, and heard Lydia and Paul gasp behind her.

"What did I tell you?" Paul was laughing. He slapped his hands against his legs and bent to rifle around the bottles at his feet for another drink.

There were a dozen or so cars parked on the left at the edge of the field. Chrissy pulled in next to them and Paul and Lydia almost fell over themselves to get out. Chrissy leaned back into her seat with a sigh. She noticed the Sat Nav's blue loading wheel had been replaced by a frozen screen and the words 'signal lost'.

"Shit." She would just have to remember the way back to the motorway in the morning.

Chrissy climbed out, stretching and rolling her shoulders to try and shift the tension that had built up during the drive. She gulped from a warm bottle of water that had been in the door compartment and leaned against the car. The heat of the metal rose through her jeans as she watched Lydia and Paul taking drunken selfies, striking stupid poses and trying to get the oak tree in behind them.

The field was surrounded by tall pines on all sides, but on the far side the woodland was denser. The setting sun caught the edge of the canopy and glowed with the warm orange of light seen behind closed eyelids. Below this shadows gathered, a deepening darkness that thickened in the visible spaces between branch and earth. The leaves rustled their quiet applause as the breeze passed through.

Chrissy glanced back inside the car. Matt was still sat in the passenger seat turning the flower over in his hands. A trickle of blood-red sap coated his fingertips. He chucked it out onto the grass and climbed out.

"St John's Wort."

"Hmm?" Chrissy offered him the bottle of water and he used it to rinse his hands before having a drink.

"The flower. St John's Wort. It's used as a herbal remedy." He paused and she could sense he was expecting her to ask how he knew, so she said nothing. "Fun fact. It's also called Demon Chaser."

She laughed. "Wonderful." As if this wasn't weird enough.

The four of them walked towards where the festival was pitched. A couple of ancient fairground rides with garish paintwork stood out alongside the carefully proportioned bonfires, archery targets and small wooden platforms. A handful of people drifted through the trampled grass. Not exactly a party; it felt haphazard and disjointed as if it had sprung up, weed-like from the earth. Everything was adorned in flowers or leafy branches and at the centre of it all was the oak tree. It was an ancient thing, stood on what might have been the boundary between two fields. Its trunk was bent with age, the bark cracked in wide fissures. Its twisted branches stretched out above the long grass, grasping for the earth rather than the sky.

A man and a woman, dressed in simple clothes, sat on fold-out chairs manning the makeshift entrance. The pair were chatting, and as the four friends approached, they stood and pulled masks down over their faces before Chrissy could see their features properly, transforming themselves into a wolf and a fox.

They stood before a table piled with rolls of brightly coloured ribbon and stacks of plastic animal masks.

"Welcome to the realm of the Oak King." The wolf greeted them with his arms wide. "Please." He gestured towards a thick row of flowers lying across the grass. "You are invited to cross the threshold."

As they shuffled over the flowers, Chrissy studied the pair's masks. Far more elaborate than their plastic counterparts, they were textured with fake fur that was sleek but worn at the edges. The shape of the eye and mouth holes seemed oddly proportioned for human faces, and the wolf's rubbery nose glistened in the sun. Lydia stepped forward with her hand raised to stroke the wolf mask and the man took a polite step back. Lydia stopped short and giggled to hide her disappointment. She turned to Paul.

"They look so real," she said. Paul hugged her from behind and rested his chin on her shoulder.

"They are pretty awesome, right?"

The fox moved around the table and held out a mask and a roll of ribbon to each of them. Her long strawberry blonde hair cascaded out from the edges of her mask, blending with the faded fur.

Chrissy met her green eyes for a second as she took the fox's offering. "Thank you."

The wolf and the fox waited in silence for them to put on their masks. When the fox spoke her voice was serious. "The Oak King resides." She pointed to the tree. "Bind yourself and be rewarded."

She pressed something into each of their hands in turn – a carved wooden circle with a strange asymmetric symbol burnt into the wood – then stepped back so that she was standing next to the wolf. They both lifted their masks together, smiling.

"Have fun guys," the man said. "And make sure you stick around until sunrise."

"The transference ceremony is not to be missed." The woman pointed to the wooden tokens in their hands. "One of you could be the lucky..." she paused as if forgetting the right word, "...winner." Her smile widened.

Chrissy realised she'd been holding her breath. It was just theatre. As they moved over towards the tree, she looked back. There were more people arriving and the fox and the wolf were repeating their bit.

The sun-bleached grass that surrounded the oak tree had been mown in a wide circle. Freshly cut logs large enough to sit on were positioned at intervals, and in front of each one a circle of grass had been peeled away like skin to reveal the earth beneath. People were still setting up, building small campfires in the circles of bare earth as the sun set behind them. Chrissy watched as twilight settled over the fields, softening everything at the edges. Above her head, the oak's branches became cracks in a bruising sky. So this is where they would gather to watch the sun rise, and witness the transference ceremony, whatever that was.

There were ribbons already tied into the tree, floating in patchy ripples of colour. Two women in denim shorts and crop tops were tying theirs around one of the lower branches close to the tree trunk, and the four friends instinctively looked for a space where they could hang their ribbons close together.

"I wonder what the prize is." Lydia bounced on the balls of her feet as she watched Paul tie her yellow ribbon onto one of the oak tree's branches. "Do you think I'll win? I never seem to win anything."

"Well if I win, I'll give it to you," Paul said. Lydia smiled and threw her arms around him. Chrissy and Matt shared a look from behind their masks.

"It's too hot for these things." Matt lifted his mask away from his face and wiped a hand across his forehead. Chrissy nodded. She took hers off and looked at it: a brown cow with thick cartoon eyelashes.

"What's yours meant to be?" Matt's mask was black with wide-set eyeholes, the suggestion of a snout and the nubs of horns in the raised plastic.

"A goat, maybe?"

❖

The quiet roar of the wind in the trees ripples through the audio, then subsides. The image is dark except for a soft slip of light across the left edge of the screen. There is the suggestion of form in the darkness. There is silence, then the crack of a twig, the flutter of wings. A shadow shifts across the edge of light. Hours pass.

The sound is faint at first but grows louder and more distinct over several minutes. There is a rhythm to the slow footsteps and the snap and scrape of something dragging through the undergrowth. "Over here," a voice yells. The harsh rustle of someone moving quickly towards the camera stops abruptly. There is a sharp intake of breath. "Shit." The soft hiss of radio static cuts off and the voice says "Call it off. We've found him." For a few moments there is only the sound of heavy sighs and radio static, then more footsteps. "Don't," the voice says. There is another sigh, the muffled thud and scratch of boots. "What the...? Jesus. Fuck." Another shadow moves across the slip of light. "It looks like...Where's the rest of him?" There is a pause, followed by a low groan. The scratch and shuffle of movement stops abruptly with wet, guttural retching. Several seconds pass before the first voice speaks again. "What the fuck's wrong with his face?"

Chrissy took a small bite of the burger and chewed. The meat coated the inside of her mouth, gamey and cloying. It was unpleasant, slightly sour. She swallowed, watching Paul and Lydia scoff theirs, too drunk to care. She eyed the stall where they had bought the food, a haphazard set up of grills and spits over a freshly dug fire pit. Bags of shop-bought burger buns and hot dog rolls were piled on the grass, and the man doling out the food was wearing an animal mask: a badger, grease clinging in its fur.

Chrissy noticed Matt was watching her. He held out the cone of chips he was nibbling on, but she shook her head. She looked down at her burger, trying to catch the colour of the meat in the light of the fire. There was a pale sheen, the faint smell of wet cardboard.

"Guys, I think there's something wrong with..." Chrissy looked round for a bin, her appetite suddenly non-existent.

"Aren't you going to eat that?" Lydia had the burger out of Chrissy's hand and in her mouth before she could say anything.

"Jesus, Lyds." She eyed the man in the badger mask, now with a queue of customers. He was out of earshot. "I think the meat is off."

Paul stepped closer. "Tastes fine to me."

Chrissy sighed but didn't argue. She was probably wrong anyway.

They drifted around the fields. The bonfires Chrissy had noticed earlier were all lit now and every so often she would catch the perfume of flowers as they caught the flames. The sharp smell of burning wood made her nostalgic for cold November nights, fireworks and sparklers.

They paused to watch the dancers on one of the

raised wooden platforms. They reminded Chrissy of traditional Morris dancers. Their plain clothes held none of the spectacle, but their movements were more intricate, almost mesmeric. The music was upbeat, with musicians playing flutes and drums, and a number of the dancers shaking bells wildly above their heads. A man with an acoustic guitar sat on the edge of the platform singing words Chrissy could barely hear over the fairground rides behind them. The tune was vaguely familiar. Something about a tree and a grave. She shivered.

Lydia leaned over and shouted in Chrissy's ear. "I could never do that. They're pretty good, aren't they?" Chrissy made herself smile. She felt a hand on her shoulder and jumped.

"You alright?" Matt asked.

Chrissy nodded. "Sorry, miles away."

"Paul's found a shooting gallery. He's so drunk he can't shoot straight." Matt was grinning. "He's spending all his money."

Chrissy took Lydia's hand and pulled her away.

The pellet grazed the side of the can, shunting it backwards, but it didn't fall.

"Damn it." Paul lowered the gun and glared at the two tin cans still standing in the stack. He fished another fiver from his back pocket and slapped it down on the counter. A man in a hare mask moved to re-stack the cans. The five pound note disappeared into the front pocket of his stained leather apron and he stepped back, tilting his head to indicate Paul could go again. There was something disjointed in the way the mask twitched above his heavy-set shoulders.

"Third time lucky." Paul raised the gun again. They watched as he worked through his four shots. There were two cans left standing.

"This bloody thing's rigged." He slammed the gun back down on the counter. The small circle of people who had been watching his attempts mumbled amongst themselves and moved off. Lydia looked from the row of stuffed animals hanging against the back wall of the booth to the bottle of beer in her hand. Paul pulled her in for a hug and kissed the top of her head.

"Where were the archery targets we saw earlier? They can't rig arrows, can they?"

He wasn't going to let this go. Chrissy started to follow them back into the crowd and realised Matt wasn't behind her. She looked back and Matt had the gun in his hand. He fired off the first shot and it missed. Chrissy watched him as he looked up, readjusted his aim and took the shot again. Four of the six cans toppled over. She didn't need to see the rest to know he'd shot them all down. Within moments he'd caught up with them, a stuffed rabbit in his hand.

"How the...?" Paul looked incredulous.

"You were right, it was rigged. Weighted to one side." Matt held out the rabbit to Lydia.

"Ah, thank you, Matt. That's super sweet." She waved the rabbit at Paul. "Look."

"Yeah, thanks Matt." Paul glared at him, then turned and walked away.

Lydia stood gazing down at the rabbit, squeezing it in both hands. It was a scruffy-looking thing, far less cute than it had seemed hanging in the booth. Chrissy put a hand on Lydia's shoulder. Lydia was frowning.

"What's wrong?"

"It's not right."

Chrissy could barely hear her over the music and the crowds. There was a bonfire nearby, the heaviness of burnt wood masking an odour Chrissy couldn't place. The fire's light flickered across the rabbit's fur and glinted in its eyes. Lydia thrust the thing into Chrissy's hands with a surprised shriek and Chrissy almost dropped it.

She felt it then – the greasiness in its fur, the soft shudder beneath her fingers as she squeezed its body. The rabbit was oddly proportioned, distorted, its fur thin and patchy in places. A seam ran the length of its belly and Chrissy traced it with her thumb. She felt something move against her skin and jerked her hand away. The rabbit fell to the grass; Lydia screamed.

Chrissy pulled her away as the maggots writhed onto the grass. She caught the shimmer of red ribbon stitched into the fur. As Matt brought his foot down the smell of decay bloomed into the air. He grunted with the effort of stamping until the crunch of bone had disintegrated into a muted squelch.

Lydia lurched away into the shadows and doubled over. Chrissy got there just in time to hold Lydia's hair out of her face as she threw up. Matt staggered back, his face full of confusion and anger. He stared back at the shooting range.

"Matt, don't." Chrissy looked around at the people watching them. No one would meet her eyes. "Leave it. Let's just go and find Paul and get out of here." Matt hovered, rubbing the back of his neck with both hands. Finally, he nodded.

They sat on the grass beneath the oak tree, huddled around an open fire. At some point in the early hours, the crowd of festival goers had drifted towards the oak tree, following an unspoken command to gather and wait. Lydia had refused to go home. The look on Paul's face might have had something to do with it. Now she leaned against him, gazing into the blue light of her phone and wrapped in the old woollen blanket they'd found waiting by the fire pit. Chrissy shook it to within an inch of its life before she let Lydia anywhere near it, the sight of maggots flexing in the grass still in her mind.

Beyond the circle of campfires, the noise and colour of the festival had fallen silent and faded into the darkness. The bonfires had all but burnt out, their dying embers glowing like clusters of watchful eyes. The odd line of softly sung folk songs drifted over, inviting sleep.

Orange yellow flames writhe across the screen. The camera zooms in and out. Chrissy is sat with her knees brought up to her chest. She is poking at the edges of the fire with a stick. There is a cracking sound as one of the logs splits open. Chrissy looks up into the camera and smiles. There are shadows under her eyes. "You ok?" She mouths the words and the screen

shudders. Lydia's left hand appears making the OK sign in front of the lens before disappearing off screen again. The edge of another fire is partially visible in the top left corner of the screen. Beyond that there is only darkness undulating through the pixels. The rumble of the wind through the trees swells through the audio.

Chrissy gazed back through the flames at the oak tree directly ahead of them, its branches heaving silhouettes against a black sky. Creeping shadows caused its shape to shift in the darkness, the swell of the ribbons like the deliberate drift of a slow dance at a wedding. Lydia's words kept replaying in her head. It's not right.

The camera pans left. Matt is sat cross-legged, leaning over the book in his lap. The shot holds on him as he turns the page, then zooms in on his hands and his arms. The hairs on his forearms are standing up. He is wearing a faded grey t-shirt, the logo obscured by his position. Only the tip of a wing is visible. The screen shifts sharply, goes dark, loses and regains focus. There is a rustling as Lydia shifts position. The camera pans up. Paul is balancing a half-empty bottle of beer between his knees. His hand moves in quick, deliberate movements as he sharpens a stick with his pocket knife. He pauses and glances at Matt before refocussing his attention on the knife. His eyes flicker towards the camera but he doesn't smile. Lydia's soft breathing is audible. The screen goes dark.

She noticed them just before dawn, their forms solidifying with the growing light like creatures that had slipped into reality from her troubled sleep. They stood in a wide circle that surrounded the campsite, all facing the oak tree, still and silent. Their features in shadow, Chrissy identified them by the profile of their faces, the shape of their ears. The fox and the wolf and the hare were among them.

A single drum beat boomed low in the half light.

Chrissy jumped.

Matt looked up, twisting on stiff limbs to see what was going on. He raised an eyebrow.

"The sun is about to come up." Chrissy gazed at the lightening sky through the oak tree's branches. "Time to meet the Oak King, I guess."

There was another drum beat and another and another, developing into a slow, deliberate rhythm. The Masks began to walk towards the tree, their steps matching the beat of the drum. They were all wearing the same plain cotton robes that trailed through the dew-laden grass. There was a symbol marked crudely on their chests that Chrissy couldn't quite make out. Not one of them looked down at the sleepy festival-goers as they walked between the campfires. A few people were waking now, rubbing sleep from their eyes and mumbling their confusion. Once level with the edge of the oak tree's twisted canopy, the masks turned to face the crowd and Chrissy could see the symbol clearly. Two triangles, one inverted and overlapping the other, the diamond at the centre forming the shape of an eye.

Paul stretched and yawned, oblivious. Chrissy shot him a look and he turned to see the Masks. Suddenly animated, he shook Lydia's shoulder. "Wake up, Lyds. Some proper old-school shit is about to go down."

Lydia blinked awake and reached for the near empty bottle of water on the grass beside her. Her sleepy smile turned into a grimace. Chrissy smiled in sympathy. She wouldn't be the only one with a hangover.

Chrissy felt Matt kneel beside her. He was turning a wooden token in his hand and Chrissy remembered the fox had given one to each of them the night before. She fished hers out of her jeans pocket, glancing from the robes to her token. The symbols were different. Then Matt held his out for her to see. She felt her chest tighten.

"It's just a bit of fun." He smiled.

Chrissy nodded and tried to return the smile. He was right. Of course he was.

They watched as the masks began to sway as if mesmerised. Then the drum fell silent. Chrissy held her breath and felt Matt squeeze her hand.

The sun broke over the horizon, a swell of light that carried the promise of warmth. The air shifted and the drum started up again, its rhythm lively and inviting. The masks started to clap to the beat, moving through the ribbons with deliberate steps and pulling them forward in offering to the crowd. Encouraged, a handful of people stood, whooping and cheering. Grabbing for their own masks, they stumbled forward still half-drunk to take their positions.

Paul rose to his feet and held out his hand to help Lydia up. Chrissy and Matt watched them go.

Paul looked back over his shoulder. "Don't be losers, get your arses over here."

Then the fox was beside them. She tilted her head to one side as she peered down at them, eyes unblinking. There was a wreath of twisted branches in her gloved hands, swollen with vibrant oak leaves and those yellow, star-shaped flowers. Chrissy and Matt stood up, their legs stiff and awkward after kneeling. Matt took an instinctive step forward to put himself between Chrissy and the fox. Chrissy became conscious of the silence. She glanced over her shoulder towards the oak tree. Everyone had taken their place. They were waiting. The Masks were scattered amongst the crowd, the edges of their robes glowing in the first spears of light from the sun. She couldn't see Paul or Lydia in the mass of plastic features and dishevelled clothes. There was a single red ribbon that had been left to hang from the tree. Hers. Wait, where was Matt's? She felt the flutter of panic in her chest before she spotted Lydia standing close by, ribbon in one hand, phone in the other.

Chrissy heard the fox speak but didn't catch her words. She turned back in time to see her crown Matt with the wreath.

"The Oak King abides." A single, harsh clap shattered the silence.

"The Oak King abides," they repeated as one. The fox turned and started back towards the tree. With each step, a clap from the crowd reverberated around the field, echoed back by the trees with the rhythm of a heartbeat.

"Don't worry, Chris. It's just for show," Matt

whispered. He held out a hand for her. Chrissy could feel the weight of everyone watching her. She bent to retrieve her mask from the grass and pulled it on. The breathy stench of something rotten drifted up at her face and caught in her throat. A second later it was gone.

Chrissy wrapped the end of the ribbon around her left hand. She clapped along and tried to catch Paul and Lydia's attention. Paul was absorbed with watching the fox whisper instructions in Matt's ear. Lydia gave Chrissy a little wave between claps and their eyes met. Chrissy smiled and then realised the mask covered her face. She waved back.

As she moved back a few steps into position, Chrissy saw the extent of the oak tree's twisted trunk. A deep gash ran the length of it, leaving a cavity in the body of the tree that was large enough for a person to slip into. She felt her stomach lurch as she watched Matt shuffle inside. *Stop it.* She just needed to lighten up and have fun.

A horn sounded across the field from the tree line. The drum beat started up again and the Masks began to dance in circles around the tree, guiding the crowd's steps and the patterns of the ribbons as they bound together.

They danced as the sun rose in the sky, laughing and cheering at their awkwardness as they learned the steps. The oak's branches seemed to swell with light above their heads, the ribbons embracing them in a cocoon of movement and colour. As she passed the gap where Matt had slipped into the body of the tree, she saw him smiling. He caught her eye and gave her a thumbs up.

She let go then, revelled in the joy of being part of something other. In the middle of the mass tangle of bodies she caught glimpses of the blue seeping back in the sky, of the sun's hazy brightness, and of their shadows writhing across the grass. There were flashes of the night before: greasy fur, the remnants of the festival, maggots, and the Masks staring from a distance, watching. The ribbons crept down the oak's trunk as they danced faster, sealing Matt inside.

The screen tumbles about with movement, swinging in wide arcs that take in a kaleidoscope of colour. A tangle of indistinct limbs shift in and out of focus, bright t-shirts, denim and bare skin, trampled grass, tree branches, a figure watching from a distance. Laughing and cheering can be heard over the shuffle of a hand over the microphone. Warm sunlight blooms across the screen before the camera is jerked down again. There is a low rumble on the audio. Then someone screams.

The scream stretches out for several seconds before yelling and shrieking drowns it out. The camera tumbles backwards and up to show Lydia's shocked face. She moves out of view and the screen is obscured for a moment as she grabs for her dropped phone. There is a glancing view of the field, of people running.

When the screen is righted it is pointed at the oak tree. The scream has stopped and Lydia is breathing heavily into the microphone. The tree's trunk is a haphazard knot of vivid colour. The camera pans slightly to the right. Chrissy is standing a few feet ahead, unmoving. "Chris?" Lydia's voice is shaky. Chrissy doesn't respond. A few seconds pass before there is another scream. It is Matt's voice.

"MATT!" Chrissy screams his name. The sound hisses and distorts to a low moan. The low rumble can be heard again before the audio corrects.

The screen lurches and pans round. Paul is pulling at Lydia's free hand, his face twisted with fear. His lips move but there are no words. The camera jerks again as Lydia pulls free. Chrissy is shouting as she rushes forwards. "The knife. Paul, give me the knife. For fuck's sake." She stands in front of the camera, partially obscuring the screen. "THE KNIFE." The camera jerks round to see Paul drop his pocket knife onto the grass, then shifts back so the tree is visible again. Part of the trunk bloats, straining against the ribbon before receding. Lydia's breathing quickens. The camera zooms in, the image blurring and then refocusing on Chrissy as she plunges the knife into the side of the tree.

There is a grunt as if someone has had the wind knocked out of them and the phone falls to the ground. The tree is still partially visible in the top right quarter of the frame. A sharp, high-pitched whine tears through the audio and the image vibrates as if the ground is shaking. The whine is replaced by the low rumble, slowly increasing in volume. A figure passes by the tree. The camera's image warps around it. Then it's gone.

Several minutes pass. The camera shifts focus between the oak tree and the blades of grass in the foreground. The wind can be heard in the trees. The screen rolls as someone picks up the phone. The fox peers into the camera lens, tilting her head to one side. Over her shoulder, the other Masks are standing in a row, still, silent and watching.

The screen flips a final time and there is a flash of Chrissy's prone body lying face down in the grass, plastic animal masks scattered around her. A hand covers the lens and the screen goes dark.

Midsummer Eve

Lisa Morton

The train was thirty minutes outside of Bath when Mackenzie looked out the window and saw the Horned Man.

She wasn't sure when he'd first appeared; she'd glanced up from her phone and seen him darting in and out of the woods fifty feet from the train. He was tall, dressed in some sort of furry brown costume with antlers attached to his head. The train sped past and the Horned Man fell from Mackenzie's sight. She thought he'd been...dancing? Frolicking?

Cosplay in the countryside, at the height of summer? Then she remembered: the solstice was in two days. Perhaps he was practicing for some midsummer ritual.

Except...the whole landscape outside the train looked different right now. There were no houses, no landscaped areas, no people; the rolling plain grew green and lonely, as it had once looked.

After a few seconds, the houses and berms and fences and fields returned, and Mackenzie leaned back in her seat, wiping sweat from her face. She was less concerned with what she'd just seen than with the heat; it was sweltering in both Great Britain and California, which she'd just left. The temperature outside the train was well over forty degrees; L.A. had been 110° Fahrenheit. The trees looked wilted, their leaves already fallen in mid-June. She remembered the conversations with Auntie Maeve when they'd both complained about global warming, which had broiled parts of Maeve's precious garden right out of existence; they both thought the future looked grim, as the planet fell deeper into the grip of climate change. As for the vision of the verdant, green countryside...she was used to that.

She wished she had Auntie Maeve to call right now; Maeve knew about the way Mackenzie sometimes envisioned the past.

Mackenzie had experienced these "little daydreams", as her mother called them, as long as she could remember. She'd been eight before she'd realized that not everyone saw places both as they were and as they'd once been. Growing up in Los Angeles, Mackenzie had gotten used to looking out the window of the car and seeing the 405 freeway and the urban landscape melt away to reveal the chaparral of thriving scrub oak and sagebrush. Occasionally she glimpsed the original inhabitants of Southern California, brown-skinned Tongva women who mashed acorns while the men returned from hunts with rabbits and fish. When she'd first arrived in London yesterday, she'd seen plumed Roman troops marching through muddy streets between rough buildings of straw and stone. Of course she hadn't told anyone about that; as soon as Mackenzie had learned that she saw the world differently, she'd also learned to keep that fact to herself.

Maeve, though, understood. Maeve, her grandmother's

sister, the one who had stayed in England while her kin headed for the U.S. Maeve, who Mackenzie had met at a family reunion fifteen years ago and had bonded with immediately, irrevocably.

Now Maeve was gone, dead at eighty-nine, with no children of her own left behind. Mackenzie had worried about her auntie recently – Maeve was complaining of pains in her left shoulder and chest, but refused to see a doctor. Still, she was heartbroken to hear of her aunt's passing; she'd miss their daily texts and twice-weekly calls, the photos Maeve sent of her garden, the enthusiastic responses when Mackenzie sent her audition videos.

Mackenzie abruptly bit back a sob as she thought about how she'd lied to her aunt for so long – or, perhaps, "misled" was a better word. Auntie Maeve believed her great niece was on the verge of becoming a Hollywood movie star.

She didn't know that the "auditions" and "screen tests" and "bit parts" Mackenzie showed her were all filmed by friends, or with her own phone. She'd never told Auntie Maeve the truth: that she'd been waiting tables for six years and had yet to land a single speaking role in anything bigger than a non-paying forty-seat theater production. "You're pretty enough to be as big as Julia Roberts," Auntie Maeve would say.

Mackenzie hadn't told Maeve what she'd learned: that Hollywood was full of pretty women, many of whom also had serious acting talent, which Mackenzie had recently admitted (to herself) she didn't possess.

Now it was too late; Maeve was gone. Well, maybe it

was for the best. Believing her beloved great niece would soon be a star had made Maeve happy.

Now she'd left everything to Mackenzie.

The call from the solicitors six days ago had sent Mackenzie reeling. Certainly Maeve hadn't been rich by any means, but she had a house in a village called Avonshire, near Bath, and a small bank account. Mackenzie had hung up from the call, collapsed into a chair for a few moments, called her mom ("Crazy old Maeve always did have a good heart," Mom had said), and then made arrangements to fly to London. She was able to get time off from the restaurant; Maeve's money would cover the travel. It wasn't as if she'd miss out on any real auditions. And she and David had split up three months ago, after two years of...well, she couldn't even call it a relationship. It was more a space-holder.

The terrain outside the train window changed, becoming less open plain with occasional copse and more rows of houses; checking her phone, Mackenzie saw that they'd be pulling into Bath station in fifteen minutes. From there, she'd connect with the solicitor and then have a twenty-minute ride to Maeve's house.

Her house now.

She wondered what she'd find in the house. She'd glimpsed Maeve's life in photographs and Skype calls, but had no idea beyond that.

It was late afternoon as the train pulled into Bath station. Mackenzie grabbed her roller-bag and her shoulder-purse, wincing in the heat as stepped down from the train. She spotted a well-dressed middle-aged woman walking up to her, smiling. "Mackenzie Quinn?"

She recognized the solicitor – Elizabeth Curwen – from her website. They shook hands, and then Elizabeth took the roller-bag and led the way to her car. Mackenzie was as thankful for the air conditioning as the solicitor's friendly manner.

The ride through Bath left Mackenzie more aware than ever of the *history* she was surrounded by. As they left the shores of the River Avon, Elizabeth drove past the Circus, with its semi-circle of eighteenth-century houses in the local yellow stone, and its association with the works of Jane Austen. Before that, the Romans had built their famed baths nearby. L.A. had still been native Tongva settlements when Bath was already a thriving city.

They dropped in briefly at Elizabeth's office, where they completed some paperwork before Elizabeth handed Mackenzie the keys. "I'm very sorry for your loss," the solicitor said, and Mackenzie thought it was sincere.

Returning to the car, they headed south out of Bath, soon leaving the city behind for tilled fields and occasional villages. As they drove, Elizabeth turned to the young American at one point and said, "I'm sure you already know this, but your aunt was a remarkable woman – a gifted healer."

Mackenzie wasn't sure how to answer; she knew Maeve had dabbled in things like astrology and homeopathics, but had never been sure how far she'd gone. "Was she?"

"Oh, yes. I used to suffer from terrible migraines, saw regular doctors for years, but nothing helped...until

I met your aunt, that is. The day she showed up at the office to hire me, she looked right at me, said, 'I can help those headaches,' and came back a day later with some concoction or other. I've never really believed in all that, but...well, damned if it didn't work."

"...all that..." Mackenzie wondered what Elizabeth would say if she told her she could sometimes just look at a place and see exactly how it had looked in the past.

They drove the rest of the way in silence. Avonshire was like something out of an old British movie, little more than a pub, a shop, and a scattering of houses. Maeve's was on a side street; Mackenzie felt a surprising rush of emotion as the car pulled up before it. There was Maeve's flower garden, half-dead from the heat and lack of tending, in the small front yard, with a low wooden fence surrounding it; she knew the back yard was bigger and held the herb and vegetable gardens. The two-story house was over a century old and could have used a fresh coat of paint, but it was nevertheless inviting.

Elizabeth stepped out of the car, leading the way up to the front door. Mackenzie was about to follow when she froze in shock.

Maeve stood in the doorway, looking pensive. Or rather, it was a *younger* version of Maeve, a woman in her forties. She peered around her vibrant, healthy garden for a moment, pensive.

Mackenzie's started to call her Aunt's name—

Maeve vanished. The flowers were dying again, their blossoms shriveled, the leaves brown; the paint on the house was peeling, the pipes rusting. Elizabeth peered at her curiously from the front steps. "Are you all right?"

Forcing her feet to move, Mackenzie nodded. "Sorry, it's just..."

"I understand. The blasted heat doesn't help any."

Mackenzie forced down the grief and alarm the glimpse of Maeve had brought; Elizabeth was waiting. Taking the keys she'd been given out of a pocket, she found the right one, slid it into the lock, and opened the front door.

Elizabeth reached past her and flipped a light switch on the right. "The power is paid through the end of the month, but I can assist you with transferring everything over to your name...if you decide to keep the house, I mean."

"Thanks." She didn't really consider living here a possibility, but thought she might keep the house in the family, perhaps rent it out. Somehow the idea of selling it felt like a betrayal.

Mackenzie inhaled and looked around, feeling Maeve in the furnishings, the decorating, the very *air*. There was the front sitting room, with its electric hearth, television, two big bookcases and old but comfortable furnishings. Mackenzie's breath caught as she saw a framed photo of her with Maeve at the reunion, the only time they'd been together for a photo. The frame was ornate and placed at the center of the mantel above the hearth – a place of honor. Elizabeth followed Mackenzie's gaze. "Oh, that's lovely. That's the two of you...?"

"Fifteen years ago, at a family reunion."

Elizabeth abruptly turned. "I should get back – it's late, and you'd probably like to settle in. The bedrooms are upstairs, you've got my card so feel free to call or text if you need anything – oh! There was one other thing." She walked across the entryway to the dining room, which was mostly filled by a huge antique dining table and chairs; an étagère full of ornate china occupied a far wall. On the table was a handmade wooden box about the size of a large book, with an envelope atop it. Elizabeth handed the envelope to Mackenzie, who saw that it bore her name in Maeve's handwriting. "She left that for you." Before she could open it, Elizabeth gave her a hug and turned to go. "Don't forget to call if you need anything."

"I won't. Thank you for everything."

Elizabeth was gone then, and Mackenzie was alone. She opened the envelope and saw a brief note inside, also in Maeve's spidery writing: *"My dearest Mackenzie: since you're reading this, you already know everything here is yours now. But the most important thing here is not the furniture or books or even the house itself; it's what's in the box. Open it, understand, and know that it comes with my belief in you. Love, Maeve."*

Setting down the note and envelope, Mackenzie pulled the lid off the box. Inside was an ancient album, bound in unmarked brown vellum and with an intricate latch; the book was stuffed to bulging with inserted, loose pages. Undoing the latch, Mackenzie gently opened the front cover and riffled through a few of the pages. Some of the loose sheets were on paper so old that it was brittle and cracking; others were modern printouts from a computer. They all seemed to contain recipes of some sort...no, not recipes, exactly, but lists of ingredients for herbal remedies. The pages of the book itself were different, though – a family history, perhaps. Mackenzie had a hard time making out the writing, but saw that the first entry was dated 1768.

She closed the book, knowing she'd have plenty of time to go through it later; she wasn't due back in L.A. for a week. In the meantime, she was curious about the rest of the house, especially the backyard.

Maeve had often told Mackenzie about her remarkable herb garden, about how successful she'd been growing things that weren't supposed to thrive in domestic gardens. She'd once taken her phone with her out back and given Mackenzie a walking tour: "*...St. John's wort – good for depression...echinacea, build up your immune system...feverfew, works wonders with headaches...chamomile for a lovely cup of tea that'll take away your stress...*"

At the far end of the spacious, clean kitchen, still hung overhead with bunches of drying herbs, was the back door. Mackenzie unlocked it and stepped out. The rear yard was indeed much larger – large enough, in fact, to accommodate a huge, old oak tree.

Mackenzie blinked and saw that the oak tree was in fact no longer there; all that remained was a thigh-high stump covered in garden tools and watering cans. Mackenzie didn't recall seeing the tree in any of Maeve's photos or videos, so she guessed it had been cut down long ago. The rest of the yard was in a sad state of failure after two weeks in the intense heat. Herbs had browned and curled in on themselves, taller stalks had fallen, even the loamy soil looked cracked and sere. The scene left Mackenzie mournful, as if Maeve's death had come twice.

"Don't fret so, love," came a whisper from behind her.

She whirled to see Maeve there, in her 80s, as Mackenzie had mostly known her, smiling, looking right into her eyes before she simply winked out.

Mackenzie started to shake. She'd never had anyone in one of the visions look her in the eye, or whisper to her. *Maybe,* she thought, *it's not me. Maybe Maeve's come back to haunt her house.*

Oddly, that idea gave Mackenzie great comfort.

She spent the next hour choosing one of the upstairs bedrooms and making it up with the well-worn but soft linens she found in a closet, then heading down to inventory the kitchen supplies. There wasn't much left, other than the dried herbs; she decided to walk to the shop she'd spotted on the drive here.

It was a short stroll, less than fifteen minutes, and she was soon checking out. The cashier was a woman about her age, with a shaggy haircut and too much makeup; as she rang up the items, she eyed Mackenzie curiously. "Just visiting?" she finally asked.

"Oh, yes...or, not exactly. I just inherited Maeve Quinn's house. I'm her niece, Mackenzie."

The cashier stopped and openly stared...but her

mouth twitched up in a smile. "Ah! We all wondered what would happen to the house." She paused long enough to ring in the last item before saying, "We all loved your aunt, everyone in Avonshire."

Mackenzie was stunned. Somehow she'd always envisioned Maeve as the elderly recluse, the childless eccentric who was whispered about. "Oh, that's so nice to hear."

"Where are you from?"

"Los Angeles."

The cashier eyed her again, and Mackenzie suspected she was wishing she had a cigarette. Finally she said, "Los Angeles. You an actress? You're pretty enough."

Mackenzie laughed. "Good guess."

"Been in anything I might've seen?"

Mackenzie bit back the urge to say *Not unless you watch a lot of YouTube*, and instead said, "I doubt it."

The cashier gave her a total, Mackenzie paid with a credit card, and together they bagged her purchases. When they finished, Mackenzie said, "Thanks so much...sorry, I didn't get your name."

"Lizzie."

"Nice to meet you, Lizzie. I'll be here for at least a few more days, so I hope I see you again."

"Yeah, you, too."

Mackenzie was nearly out the door when Lizzie called after her, "Are you a good witch like she was?"

That stopped Mackenzie dead in her tracks. She thought for a few seconds before answering, "I'm not really sure."

It was the most truthful response she could come up with.

She spent the rest of the day relaxing in Maeve's sitting room (*her* sitting room) with tea and the box of papers. The house was hot – apparently it wasn't built for weather like this – but Mackenzie was nevertheless comfortable. Happy, even.

Most of the separate pages were recipes for cures. The journal, however, was more interesting. It had been started in 1768 by a woman named Breana, who would've been Mackenzie's many times-great grandmother. Much of it was just the recording of everyday life ("John left today for the Martinmas fair, as we'll need three stout men for the spring planting"), but there were occasional entries that were anything but everyday: "On St. John's Eve I learned that my little Henry will wed Annie Locke in ten years' time," or, "I felt the Morrigan's presence last night. It should be a fine year for harvest."

Mackenzie flipped quickly through the pages, discovering that generations of her female ancestors had added to the book. Maeve's entries started in 1982, after her mum had died.

Ten pages later Mackenzie was crying, not because her beloved aunt's life had been difficult or tragic, but because of how strongly her voice came through. In fact, as Mackenzie continued to read, she found herself envying Maeve's life, which had been full of learning and living things and friends...and *magic*. Maeve's abilities to diagnose and heal and prognosticate had far outdistanced those who'd come before. She also spoke more openly about communing with gods. She wrote of the Morrigan and the Dagda, of Danu and Lugh, and of Cernunnos, the Horned One.

Cernunnos...

Mackenzie thought about the man with antlers she'd seen on the train just a few hours ago. Was he supposed to be Cernunnos? Her aunt described the god as the protector of wild things and nature. Maeve had prayed to him, burned oils she'd made especially in his honor.

Remembering that she'd also seen the surrounding countryside's past, Mackenzie had a more disturbing thought: what if she had actually seen a horned god, a divine being who'd been worshiped here in the past?

She took a deep breath to calm herself and was about to shut the book when her own name caught her eye. She looked down – and her heart froze at what she read:

My dearest Mackenzie: you are reading this because I am gone. You've read this far, which means you're well along on your path of discovery, so it's time you learn the rest.

For generations, our women have known you were coming. The gods have promised you, even though you didn't know. You possess skills and powers you aren't even aware of. You know you can see the past of a place, but did you know you can make that past the present? Not just as a vision only you can see, but as the reality for all.

I regret not telling you this while I lived. It was nothing but cowardice. I feared what you are, even though I know you are also good and decent.

Use everything I've left you. Use it cautiously, but always know that you can make the world better.

Love, Your Maeve.

Mackenzie slammed the journal shut and tossed it aside. She rose angrily, wiping at tears. She saw now that Maeve had been delusional; she didn't know that her niece had lied to her about her acting, her failed life. Mackenzie wasn't the honest, kind person that Maeve had been, and had believed her to be as well. She certainly didn't possess "skills and powers" beyond a strong imagination. Her life, compared to Maeve's, felt empty and pointless.

Furious, she stalked through the house and out into the back. It was full night now, the moon a waning crescent sliver, the desiccated garden dead or dying beneath the stars. Mackenzie saw the stump where the oak tree had once been...

Or rather, where she saw it now, its branches spread so far that they filled the entire yard, the leaves grown thickly together and green.

"Useless," Mackenzie muttered to herself. *So I can see a fucking tree. Big deal. It's meaningless, Maeve. I'm nothing, and you were a whackjob.*

She returned to the house, found a half-full bottle of whiskey in the kitchen, and drank herself into bed.

When she awoke in the morning, head throbbing, she glanced out the bedroom window and saw:

The oak tree. It still stood exactly as she'd seen it last night.

Mackenzie, her head in agony, stumbled down the stairs, through the kitchen and out into the yard, where she felt the cool shade cast by the thick growth above. She ran a hand down the trunk, pulled it back and smelled the rich scent on her fingers.

The tree was real.

She staggered into the kitchen, rummaged through the cabinets, and found a small bottle labeled, "For headaches." She poured a few drops into a cup of boiling water, feeling better within minutes.

After examining the tree again – to assure herself it was *really* real – she went into the sitting room, intent on going through the journal for more clues.

The journal sat open on the couch. Mackenzie distinctly remembered leaving it on a nearby table.

She approached it warily, as if it might spring to life. She picked it up to read what it was open to.

It was a 1993 entry from Maeve discussing a midsummer ritual. It involved gathering materials for offerings, speaking incantations, and burning herbs to summon the spirit of Cernunnos. At the bottom of the entry were two lines written in a different color of ink:

Prepare today.

Call him tomorrow.

The writing was not only in a different color of ink (black, not blue), but there was a black pen resting nearby that Mackenzie didn't recall seeing before.

Today was the 19th of June. Tomorrow was the solstice.

Mackenzie pushed the book away, cursing her own naivete. *The tea...there was something more in it than a headache cure, now I'm imagining a lot of bullshit...this is fucking ridiculous. I was obviously right all along, and my aunt WAS a deluded eccentric.*

"Perhaps," said a voice behind her.

She turned, but there was nothing.

Thinking then of the oak tree, Mackenzie pulled out her phone and thumbed through to a photo Maeve had sent her two months ago, when the garden was in the throes of spring and a panorama of mad colors. There were the flowers in the front yard, and in the back yard, herbs in neat patches...

And the stump of the oak, with gardening implements resting on it.

Mackenzie walked with her phone to the back, took a photo of the yard, and examined it. If she was imagining the oak, so was her camera, because it showed up there, in its full, spreading glory.

Had she indeed restored the oak?

Mackenzie stood in the welcome shadow beneath the tree and thought about the dead herbs. She imagined the past of two months ago, when they'd been alive and growing.

As she watched, they transformed, like paint running off a canvas in reverse. Stems righted themselves, blossoms regained petals, fresh scents claimed the air.

Mackenzie's knees lost strength and she fell to a patch of soft, springy mint.

I did that.

She was barely surprised when she heard a whisper from behind her: "Yes, you did."

She didn't need to turn this time.

She spent the rest of that day and the evening reading the journals. There were other references to midsummer, but none of the rest had those two lines that she increasingly thought were directed to her.

Prepare today.

Call him tomorrow.

She checked online for information on the solstice; it would occur at 10:43 p.m., about an hour and twenty minutes after sunset in Great Britain. There was also a solar eclipse scheduled to occur on that day, and a new moon. Mackenzie had never believed in portents and signs, but they seemed significant this year.

Mainly out of respect for Maeve, she decided she would follow her aunt's midsummer ritual as closely as possible. She would need a cauldron of water and an offering of silver; she found a huge, ancient cast-iron pot that would serve for the former, and a nondescript ring (which she couldn't even be sure was silver) for the latter. A sacred fire would need to be made, and oils burned in it; she found a circle of stones in the backyard that she thought had probably served as a fire pit in the past, and – although she didn't know which oils would serve best – the cupboards were full of tiny stoppered vials. She needed smudge sticks of sage, which hung from the kitchen ceiling, and a "nemeton", or sacred space, preferably an oak grove. In the back she had a single tree that had been miraculously rebirthed, so she figured that would serve.

The night before, her dreams were vivid and unnerving. Mackenzie stood under the oak; it was night, impossibly black. She somehow knew that Maeve stood beside her, though when she turned she couldn't see her. The shadows just beyond the tree's spread were impenetrable, but full of whispered snarls, imprecations in a language she couldn't parse. She sensed that she was required to make a decision, but she didn't know what it should be.

She awoke too early, already covered in sweat before the sun had even edged up over the horizon, the sky violet and fervid.

The ritual Maeve had recorded included prayers to be said throughout the day of the solstice, so Mackenzie said them, even though she felt more than vaguely silly and had no idea if she was pronouncing the names (Diancecht, Tuatha de Danann) properly. She was shocked when it was still light at 8 p.m., but had to remind herself that this wasn't Los Angeles.

At 9 p.m., she began to set out the items she'd need: the cauldron (pot) of water, the ring, the oils, the pages. Lastly, she set fire to kindling she'd gathered and placed in the center of the stone ring.

At 9:26, the sun slid completely below the horizon, leaving the sky bruise-hued. Just as Maeve's rite had indicated, she began to recite the invocations that marked the real beginning of the midsummer ritual.

"I call on you, Shining Ones, to answer me and make your way forthwith. I call on the Morrigan and the Dagda, on Diancecht the great healer, on Cernunnos the Horned One, to honor my invocation and be present..."

The sky began to darken, the stars appearing, looking brighter than usual. Mackenzie knew there was an eclipse occurring on the other side of the world right now, and she glanced at her phone.

10:39

If something was going to happen, it would be in the next four minutes.

The invocation called for the silver to be offered to the water, and she placed the ring in the pot. Next, the oils were fed to the fire, which sparked and sent up curls of fragrant smoke.

10:42

The oak branches rustled, not as if shaken by a breeze but in distinct paths, as if something unseen moved there. The overheated air grew chill as a musky, woodland smell assaulted Mackenzie. She pushed sudden misgivings aside and tried to muster a shout: "I call on you, Cernunnos, to attend and bless this sacred nematon."

Mackenzie glanced down at the phone she'd left near her feet.

It was 10:43.

She waited, breathless, shivering in the unexpected cold. Her breath formed small puffs, the branches moved overhead, *that smell...*

The small fire shot up a shower of sparks, but the glowing dust didn't fall back to the ground; instead, it settled into a shape – that of a tall, horned man. Or not a man exactly...

"Cernunnos," Mackenzie breathed out. As she watched, the space outlined by the embers took on solidity and color, but the voice came from within Mackenzie's own head: *You summoned me.*

"Yes," she blurted out, wanting to add *but I didn't believe it would actually work and now I don't know what to do and I—*

You have great power.

"I don't understand," Mackenzie blurted out. "What...what am I supposed to do?"

Change.

"Change what?"

The figure above the fire wavered slightly. Then *it* – the god, the Horned One – forced more than its words into her mind, and Mackenzie saw:

It wasn't herself she could change – it was *everything.* She could take the world back twenty, fifty, a hundred, a thousand years, back before the heat that had come with mankind's tampering. She could give the earth back its *own* climate, guarantee that life would continue, and it would be *easy* – as easy as imagining it.

Change, thought Cernunnos again, and this time Mackenzie knew it was not an answer to a question, but a request. Of course: this god of wild things wanted an untamed world again.

It *would* be easy...but Mackenzie forced herself to think the act through: *If I do this, what would happen to people? To civilization?*

Gone.

Mackenzie felt feverish, sick. This was too much to ask, of her...of the world.

Save.

Not everyone would be gone – she would remain, of

course – but so many things she loved would be lost forever.

Nothing of worth.

What would she be giving up? She could probably never return to Los Angeles, but what did she have to return to? There'd be no more movies, no more internet, no more restaurant to hide a failed career in. She had no one to return to. Here she'd have a home, the work of nurturing; surely some others would remain and in time she'd have friends, a community, perhaps even love...

Choose.

Mackenze felt the matrix of the universe contract around her; all points now led to her, to this moment, to this decision.

"I will," she said. She took a deep breath and closed her eyes.

She chose.

Midsummer Eve

Stewart Hotston

The heat was stifling, beading sweat onto his upper lip and making the steering wheel slippery. Feum fiddled with the air conditioning, eventually thumping the controls on the dash in frustration. A cloud of dust bloomed into the air, catching the sunshine as it pierced the windscreen's tint.

'I'm sorry, buddy,' he told his passenger, but Solas did little more than huff in discomfort and put his head between his paws.

The drive back from the village took them twenty minutes. The roads were clear – everyone was down by the shore or deep in the woods hunting stag. Midsummer might be long but the weather it brought was fleeting, the heat and sunshine gone much quicker than the long days.

The drive up to their cabin was hazy in the warmth but under the tyres the road crunched comfortably, as solid as ever. Feum pulled up with a jerk of the handbrake. Solas strained against the motion and remained on the passenger seat but gave Feum a stare which said he put up with a lot and this wasn't the kind of thing he felt he should endure.

The warmth coming through the screen was radiant

on his hands, dry and comforting, unlike the humidity of the car. Times like these he wished he could stand in the sun, could feel it on his face without fear. Without the suncream, without the protection he needed just to walk outside without blistering and burning like bacon under a grill. Feum absently ran his hands over Solas' head, fingers through his hair, then grabbed thick black leather gloves from the top of the dash and pulled them on. Wishing wouldn't make it so.

Solas' tongue lolled in an effort to cool down.

Feum reached around to the back seat and grabbed at his wide brimmed-hat. Placing it on his head he took a breath, opened the door and stepped out into the summer sun.

Sweat trickled down from under the brim, rolling past his eye and down his cheek.

His jacket was zipped up to his neck, his chin tucked inside the high collar. From behind him he heard Solas slink from the car, nose in the air, then he was gone to read the news on the stumps, rocks and corners of the house.

It might be hot but his dog had a life to lead.

The shadows were about as short as they would get. Tomorrow was the hump. A promise the days following would get shorter and Feum's unwilling imprisonment would slowly ease, until he could luxuriate in the freedom of winter and its long careless nights.

He opened the front doors, leaving the inner mosquito netting in place while he returned to the car and unloaded supplies for the next week.

He heard Solas rooting around under the kitchen window, panting and snuffling.

'Has that fox been around again?' he called. 'Trying to muscle in on your patch?'

There was silence as Solas listened, before concluding that Feum didn't need anything and continuing on with whatever scents were occupying him. Beyond him lay the forest, silent but busy, crackling, snapping, calling but somehow swallowing the sound of its life; Feum could stare at the trunks around the house in contemplative silence for hours.

Once the shopping was away and Solas' steak dinner was resting on the kitchen counter, Feum plonked down in front of his workstation. Three wide screens, high-definition displays showing nothing more exciting than his current project. He kept one screen for personal use and mail, split half and half with the bottom right hand corner cycling through the cameras he'd installed around the house and along his boundaries. They were motion sensitive and he spent many idle moments rapt by sightings of birds and animals. He was convinced a wildcat had found its way up the gully, following tourists' summer barbeque waste, although he'd not seen anything more than suspect scat.

The other screens were given over to pitches in the centre and everything else on the right – be it spreadsheets or the legal documents which made everything possible.

It took a moment for him to remember what he'd been working on before leaving for town. A half-written email, cursor flashing vacuously. A pitch half marked up.

He remembered being irritated enough by what he knew he had to write he'd decided to go to the island's one village instead. In the middle of the day. In full sunshine.

The house was cooler than the car. An insulated slate roof helped, as did wooden walls, but actual working air conditioning throughout was the clincher.

His fingers held memories he didn't know he had. He'd long ago learned to just start writing because it would be ok – his mind would catch up and off they'd go together.

Bad news. His client was being unrealistic; they wanted all the positives without any of the drawbacks, any of the checks and balances which would leave Feum's company safe if the relationship turned sour. The relationship manager wouldn't want to hear it. They never did want to deliver difficult news to the client. He didn't blame them – only lunatics relished such encounters. It wasn't his problem, for which he was glad.

The afternoon passed with occasional wafts of warm air from outside. When Feum looked up it was to find the oversized antique wall clock, saved from a demolished railway station, showing it was after six. Reflexively he checked his watch before calling for Solas.

Nothing.

He checked the kitchen just in case the dog had been in and snaffled the steak while he was absorbed in work. He wasn't surprised to find the plate untouched. He stood looking at the steak as if it could tell him the story of his absent hound. Solas wasn't immediately visible on any of the cameras which covered his favourite places to bask in the sun.

Feum stood on his porch. The early evening was as bright as midday. The sun still high in the sky. He was continuously amazed by how the rest of the world took the long days in their stride. Birds continued to call, animals ate, moved and mated as if long days were normal. He got momentarily distracted by a bird call he didn't recognise –a cough and a caw bracketed by rising staccato chirrups. Normally he'd have recorded it, would have strained to remember it.

Instead, 'Solas!'

His foot hovered over the boards in front of the house. He called again. Nothing.

The dog could and would wander across the boundary of his land but he'd always return for dinner. And dinnertime had passed, but there was no sign of a dog driven by his stomach.

Feum went back inside, rooting around the drawer by the front door and got out his whistle. Returning to the front door he grabbed his gloves, hat and car keys.

Three short pips on the whistle and a call of 'Solas'. Then he waited.

'Where are you?' he asked quietly, scanning the trees and trying to see into the shadows. The woods seemed denser, unwelcoming without the certainty of his friend by his side.

A crack to his right.

'At last,' he said, not sure if he was going to tell Solas off or simply hug him for returning. Except it wasn't

Solas. A huge stag emerged from the treeline and stared right at him. They watched one another, still as the trees among which they were stood.

It was a beauty. He counted fourteen points and rued not having his camera to hand. The stag's ears turned away from him and then, with a snort, it moved back into the trees and out of sight.

The spell broken, Feum's stomach warned him of its concern. Solas would never have let the stag approach without barking, jumping and running about – albeit without quite knowing what he should be doing about it.

Feum donned his hat and walked over to the car. His hand on the door handle, he paused. No point driving down the road. Solas could be anywhere.

Think it through, he told himself. Hot day. Hot dog. Worth checking the gully first.

The small waterway ran along one edge of his land, separating him from his neighbour, a pharma entrepreneur who came up in winter for Christmas. He only knew that much because Janice at the store in town had told him – he'd never even seen them, let alone spoken with them.

He listened as he walked, stopped at every sound in case it was Solas running home, except the forest was a concert of its own noise. What once was familiar now strange in its failure to bring Solas his way.

The water was running low, like sweat down wrinkled skin. In winter it could stream past, white and harsh enough Solas would do little more than sniff at the edges and look on mournfully. Feum reached it after about twenty minutes hiking through the thick coniferous woodland. Spots of sunshine reached down through the trees as if pleased with their wiles, but it was nothing to worry him. The air was close but rich with the smell of sap and moist earth.

He whistled every couple of hundred metres. Solas could hear the whistle over half a kilometre away on a still day. The susurrus of the trees was soft, barely more than the hiss of a detuned radio. His stomach was slowly turning over like dug earth, revealing the worms of his fear.

He walked along the gully away from the house, towards the road, before the stream doglegged back into the wilderness. He'd walked it often enough, had followed it when it was raging and when it was frozen. He thought he knew its moods.

He walked for another fifteen minutes until he heard the sound of pounding feet, of brush being swept aside, of approaching momentum. A huge smile broke out onto his face and Feum crouched down, hands out, facing the direction of the noise.

Solas burst from the undergrowth, tongue hanging out, ears flat back and eyes fixed on Feum. He bounded in, nose touching his master's outstretched palm.

'Good boy,' said Feum, all thoughts of reprimand gone like the last snowfall of spring under sudden sunshine. Solas squirmed with pleasure under his vigorous stroking, weaving between his legs then backing away to bark at him.

'I know,' said Feum, thinking they were both pleased to see one another. 'Shall we go home?' He turned to start the walk back. 'With me.'

'Is he yours?' asked a voice.

Feum stopped. A young boy, couldn't be more than twelve, was standing a few feet away in the exact place from which Solas had emerged.

'Yes,' he said warily. What was a kid doing out here? His neighbour was an old divorced white guy with grown up children and a girlfriend half his age. A walking cliché. The other side of Feum was managed forest, logging country. Not family friendly.

There weren't any kids on the island these days – the last families had moved back to mainland Scotland a decade ago. Especially ones with brown skin and leaves in their unruly hair.

'He's lovely,' said the kid. 'I was calling him Sunshine.'

Feum looked down at Solas and his golden coat. 'That's not his name.'

The kid looked at him as if to ask what it actually was, but Feum didn't want to tell him. What had he been doing playing with an obviously lost dog?

'Are you lost?' he asked slowly.

The kid shrugged. 'I like playing out here. Feels like no one is around. There are always people around. Sometimes I like being alone?' he finished up as if seeking Feum's understanding.

'You shouldn't be out here on your own,' he said. He opened his mouth to give the talk about strangers, then saw the irony and shut up again.

'Are you here on holiday? Where are your parents?'

The boy shook his head and Feum caught a whiff of lime. He wanted to sneeze, to take a step back. Limes worsened his allergic reaction to sunshine. Was it the boy who smelled that way?

'Can I take you home?' he asked.

'Can I play with him again?' asked the boy.

Solas was sniffing the bole of a tree, unconcerned by either of them.

'If you let me take you back maybe we can arrange it with your parents? I can give them my address.'

'I know where you live,' said the boy blithely. 'He doesn't have enough company. Dogs are pack animals, and all you do is sit inside in the dark.'

The words sounded so implausibly real that Feum ignored them at first. 'What were you doing with my dog?'

'Running with him. Showing him where the rabbits are burrowing and how to avoid the wildcat. It's very grumpy and he'd lose the argument.'

Feum felt stabbing shards of jealousy. He didn't run. He'd never been one for it, but he longed to take Solas further afield, to explore in the winter when they would have no cares about the climate being their enemy.

'Why do you sit in the dark?' asked the kid.

Feum wanted to know who the boy was – he wanted to ask his parents what they thought of him spying on strangers.

It's not safe, he thought. It was how he'd explain it to them, how he'd get them to stop the child trespassing without sounding like a dick about it.

'Where do you live?' he asked. Try as he might, he knew he sounded angry. He wanted to be friendly, to take a step back and start again.

'I'm not telling you,' said the boy defensively. 'Everyone knows it's not sensible to talk to strange men.' The smell of lime again, like the kid had bathed in fruit juice.

Feum remembered being scared of adults at that age. This one seemed confident, self-assured.

Maybe it was time to take Solas and get home.

'Well say hello to your parents from me.'

'Can I play with him again?' asked the boy to his back.

'No,' said Feum without turning.

'Why not?' called the kid.

Feum didn't answer.

'Mister. Why can't I play with him again? He wants to play with me. Sunshine!'

At his side Solas stopped walking and faced the boy, tail raised.

Feum was done. 'Look,' he said, turning back to face the boy. 'This is my dog. I asked you to bring your parents over so we could talk and then we could see but you've been rude and have refused to even give me your name. You could see he was lost, and you didn't do anything about it.' He threw his hands down. 'I'm not having this conversation with a child.'

'You weren't going to let me play with him. You were going to tell them to stop me coming round. You have all this beauty around you, a place unspoiled by your kind in which to be,' said the boy as Feum walked away. 'But it hasn't made you nice.'

'I'm perfectly nice,' said Feum as he climbed over a fallen tree, his heart pumping at the boy's words. 'Come on, Solas, let's get you dinner.'

'You don't deserve him,' shouted the kid as they separated. 'He needs proper friends.'

People taking other people's dogs are not good friends, he wanted to shout back. He even stopped to say it. Except stood there in the shade he knew he was being ridiculous, arguing with a child. If someone heard them, if the boy told his parents, he could only come off badly.

And what had he meant by 'your kind'? Where had he heard that kind of phrase?

They got back to the house and Solas scoffed down the steak without it touching the sides before curling up at the front door and falling asleep.

Feum sat by him for a while, back against the wall, knees raised up, hand slowly ruffling the dog's hair.

'Did I overreact?' he asked the sleeping hound. 'He was only a boy. He should have brought you back.' He thought about what he would have done at that age and confusing images and ideas came flooding through. He wanted to believe he'd have done the right thing, but he couldn't really remember being that young, and what he could recall involved a life of stricter tedium than playing unsupervised in the woods.

'There weren't woods where I lived,' he told Solas. He hadn't had a garden. Windows behind blackout blinds were his only escape, Glasgow streets into which he wasn't allowed to go, filled with fumes, shouts and horns. He rubbed at old scar tissue on the top of his ears where he'd learnt the hard way to listen to his parents.

Other children didn't care how he'd managed to sneak out, all they wanted was to see if he really burned if the sun touched his skin.

'It's why I love being up here with you,' he said. Solas stretched out, checked Feum was still there with tired eyes and settled back down. 'We get out enough, don't we?'

Sighing, he wished the encounter had played out differently. 'I was a dick,' he said to the air. He imagined playing with the kid, the two of them bonding over their love of Solas. He could have been a friend. Instead he'd pushed the boy away, excluded him. He sighed and decided he needed to eat. Staring out through the gaps in the venetian blinds across the yard, he made dinner.

The house was surrounded by the ancient trees he'd refused to chop down when the construction company had built his lodge. He loved them for their age and for how they offered him the option of being outside during the day without risking exposure to sunlight. They took the place of his parents, the branches stretching over him protectively, safety found under their canopies.

The day was still bright when he went to bed, Solas laid out, head between paws at the foot of the bed. He'd made his peace with the perpetual daylight of summer years ago.

He groaned and rolled over. Light was peeking around the blinds, although not enough to disturb him and, at this time of year, not enough to tell whether it was early or late. He checked his phone and saw it was after eight. He jerked upright, looking around for the dog. At the back of his mind something yawed, deep and fearful.

'Solas, has someone slit your throat?' He was used to being woken by the groans of a dog who wanted feeding at seven on the dot and made sure he knew it too.

The bedroom door was open. No sound of the dog in the house beyond. Everything felt empty.

Feum puzzled over whether he'd left the front door open. Maybe the dog had let himself out. Except he always wanted food at seven.

After the scare the day before, Feum threw on a long-sleeved t-shirt and jeans before padding out to the front door.

Which was open. There was a smell of lime zest in the hallway. Hand on the latch, the door swung closed then open as he looked out into the sunshine beyond.

'Shit.' He darted back to the bedroom, chest tight, unable to focus. He grabbed his sunglasses, a baseball cap and thin gloves.

Back at the front door, he thought *That fucking kid*.

He pulled a bottle of suntan cream from a drawer. He squeezed out a blob the size of a baby sprout before spreading it across his hands and the back of his neck, up to the base of his hair. Sides of his ears, the lobes, the tip of his nose and his chin.

The last layer of armour – his lightest wind cheater, the one with the collar which zipped up to his nose.

He took a look in the mirror, made sure his skin glistened in all the right places, then stepped out.

The sky was stark blue, bright as a bulb. The shadows

were short already. He pulled the collar up on his jacket and started directly for where he'd found Solas the day before. In his mind he knew the boy had come, had taken the dog away.

Hadn't he threatened as much?

The route seemed easier, as if the trees had shifted in the night, decided they'd been too close to one another and made room to enjoy the sun without competition from their neighbours. The lacunae slowed him down, made him pause as if he were playing a game of *don't step on the cracks.* Sunshine found the leaf-littered ground and Feum's feet crackled as he walked.

He heard human voices ahead. Then a dog barking. He picked up the pace, refraining from running only because the sweat dripping down his forehead was running into his eyes.

He didn't see the boy at first. He burst into a clearing by the gully and it stopped him short. He was sure there hadn't been one here before. He'd lived there long enough to explore every part of his land and the surrounding area. The forest was ancient, unmanaged as it ran up into the mountains. The one thing it definitively *wasn't* was filled with clearings forty feet across, in which young women with red hair and pale skin stood in long flowing dresses, watching him back with clear dark eyes.

He stared at the glade as if it were an illusion he could dispel by disbelieving in it. He'd walked through this exact spot the day before. The trees hadn't been chopped down – they simply weren't there anymore. Grass and wildflowers grew as if they'd spent all season soaking up the sun. Bumblebees and butterflies dawdled in the warmth, picking their way from flower to flower.

He found he couldn't look away. Her expression was so open, so mild, he thought she might be vulnerability come to life. She was the type of person he'd want to have a picture of on pitches about environmental legislation, or perhaps speaking on behalf of a left-wing super PAC hoping to strengthen climate change policies.

'It's him,' said a voice he knew. The boy was at the edge of the clearing with another child, shorter and younger than him. He struggled to work out if they were a boy or a girl. They wore dungarees, and their face refused to give away the indicators he was trying to spot.

Solas was with them, nosing about at the smaller child's closed hands.

Feum called him. Solas barked but didn't come, instead sitting down next to the boy.

'Sunshine's just playing,' said the woman, and her voice sounded like a young tree which had just survived its first frosts.

'His name is Solas,' said Feum. His voice sounded like gravel in his ears and he felt small saying the words. *Except they're true,* he thought.

The girl nodded as if his words confirmed something she already suspected. 'My brother said you were mean to him. This isn't a place where you can get away with human cruelty.'

He stared at them incredulously. 'You're not related,'

he accused, and even as he said the words he felt the ground slipping away.

'Why do you always wear winter clothes?' asked the youngest. 'Aren't you hot? Don't the seasons touch you?'

The expression on the elder girl's face told him she wanted to speak, but she looked at the youngest and then at him as if he needed to address that first.

'Direct sunshine hurts my skin,' he said.

'Unnatural like a vampire,' said the boy with relish.

Feum sighed. A comment heard without number which only made him more irritable. 'Except I'm real. It's made worse by environmental factors, like hogweed and parsley.' *And lime,* he thought.

'Does it hurt?' asked the youngest.

'Sometimes,' he said. 'Better too hot than burnt.'

'Would you burn now?' asked the boy. In his eyes Feum saw the same analysis as in every bully he'd encountered. He felt seen as a puzzle to break, a balloon to burst.

In spite of himself, Feum gazed up at the sky. He nodded at them.

'I've got to take Solas home now.' He felt calmer, less angry, but could feel his world shifting dangerously and wanted to get away.

'Why would you say we weren't related?' asked the girl.

The words caught in his throat. They weren't the same colour. She was as pale as they came but the boy was hazelnut, a beautiful colour but nothing like her. Feum considered the third of them. They were darker too, their hair shaved so he couldn't tell what was going on there.

What am I doing? he thought. He really didn't want to answer her.

'Is it because we're different colours?' asked the youngest.

He didn't answer them.

'Some people think they can tell because our skin's different,' they continued, their voice piercing in the empty clearing. 'My sister says they're helpfully revealing their ignorance. Nature does not care for your prejudices. Some maple have red leaves, others green. Do you say they can't be related?'

The girl nodded, satisfied she'd been quoted accurately, and stared hard at Feum.

'So is it because you're a racist?'

'I'd just like to take my dog and go home,' he said, tired and fearful. 'I didn't mean anything by it.' He knew whatever else he said would land him further into deep waters from which he already sensed he couldn't easily escape.

'Sunshine doesn't want to go with you,' said the boy, hand on the dog's collar.

'He doesn't get to choose,' said Feum angrily.

'Why not?' asked the girl, her voice level, quiet but with an authority he knew he needed to respond to. 'All animals make their own choices. Who are you to say he can't make his?'

'He's a dog. He's *my* dog.' He'd had enough. He strode towards the boy who watched him come over with narrowed eyes. Solas watched him too but didn't make a move to meet halfway.

'C'mon boy,' he said, but Solas didn't move. He stood

there feeling like a fool. He tried again but although he had Solas' attention, the dog stayed by the boy's side.

Frustrated, Feum grabbed Solas by the collar. 'We're going home, mate.' Solas jumped to his feet and came.

'You're hurting him,' said the boy.

Feum ignored him but let go of Solas, who immediately stopped walking. Feum wanted to shout. He wanted to plead with Solas to show them they belonged together. Normally he would have had treats on him, could have enticed the dog, but he'd left the house without, hadn't thought he'd need to persuade his own dog to come home.

'It's breakfast time,' was the best he could manage.

'You should leave him,' said the girl. 'He doesn't want to go with you.'

'He's happy here, walking between the trunks of our kin,' said the boy.

Feum grabbed at his collar again and the dog started walking. His mind swirled at the boy's words, terrified at what he didn't know.

'My brother was right,' said the girl. 'You really are very mean.'

Feum was petrified they'd follow him, but as he checked over his shoulder, he saw them staying in the glade, staring after him.

After a while he let go of Solas' collar and the dog walked along at his side.

'Now you walk with me,' he said, relieved in spite of it all.

The woodland was thinner than he remembered. For a moment he thought he was lost. Except he'd walked that way a hundred times with Solas. He knew the route home in the sun, in the rain, in the dark and in the snow. He could have closed his eyes and made it back.

Yet the woodland was thinner still. As if the trees had hitched up their skirts and stepped away from one another. The path which had been mottled with sunlight earlier was now clear of trees completely. Sunshine gave the earth a warm reddish tint.

They turned away from the gully to cut across home.

Feum stopped at the edge of the trees, a boundary which hadn't existed when he'd rushed from the house earlier. His cabin was an island in a sea of grass. The forest, which had come up against the porch when he'd left an hour before, was gone. Instead, for fifty feet in every direction, there was only ankle-high grass.

His heart lurched. Feum wiped his gloved hand across his forehead. It was just like the glade where he'd come across the children playing with Solas. He wanted to swallow, to blink and have everything return to normal.

Except the trees were gone, and with them went his sense of the forest being a place of safety.

Feum didn't dare cross the gap.

Solas, bored, leapt out into the space between the trees and their house. Feum called after him but didn't persist when he saw the dog happily sniffing around.

The moment of panic gave way to a sense of foolishness. The dog padded across the grass, tail raised high, nose to the dirt, darting one way then another. Oblivious.

Feum shook his head, dismissing his unease, and

walked across the grass to the house. Nothing bad happened.

❖

He spent the rest of the day unable to concentrate on work. Giving it up as a lost cause, he played with Solas and cooked steak on the barbeque under a big parasol.

He wanted to sleep but couldn't. The midsummer sun was going to be in the sky through to the next day. At least it would start improving from tomorrow.

In a month we'll get proper night again, he thought ruefully.

Sat on his porch, onto his fourth beer, he suddenly hated it all. He wanted to be elsewhere, where the sun wouldn't be so ubiquitous, so able to imprison him.

And where had the fucking trees gone? He took his gloves off, happy the shade protected him from the constant threat of being outside.

He had an urge to get in the car and drive south until he found night properly.

He stepped down off the porch into the summer sun. Hands were thrust into pockets, but he could feel the heat on the skin around his cuffs. He stopped, considered turning back to get his gloves.

Fuck it, he thought.

Solas watched him from the porch.

He got to the truck and stood there dumbfounded. At first he thought he'd parked in a particularly soft patch of ground but when he was stood next to it he could see roots had broken up through the ground and wrapped themselves around the wheels.

He crouched down onto the earth and checked under the car, knowing already what he was going to see. The same branches, some as thick as his wrist, had entwined themselves around the axle.

Getting back to his feet he rubbed at his wrists, then caught himself doing it.

He scurried back to the porch and the safety it offered. His wrists were blistering. He could see them swell as liquid pulsed under the skin where sunlight had touched him.

He didn't understand. He could survive a few minutes without consequence, and it was nearly eleven at night. Even on midsummer day the light was weak; a golden treacle of a sunset which never came, far from the intensity of the midday sun.

He rushed inside the house and found his antihistamines.

Solas was barking.

What now? he thought tiredly.

Feum swallowed the pills down and rambled back outside, trying not to pick at the blisters on his wrists. He couldn't put the gloves on now, couldn't let them rub against his injuries.

'Solas,' he called as he stepped out into the sun. The trees had, if anything, moved further back. He was beyond caring.

Solas was ahead tugging on a stick held by the boy.

'Get off my land,' shouted Feum, running at them. Solas saw him coming and ran from the boy to greet him.

Gritting his teeth in triumph he stared down at the boy.

'We only wanted to play with him,' said the girl, appearing at the treeline off to his left.

'You should have let us play with him,' said the boy, swinging the stick around like a baseball bat.

'I'm calling the police,' said Feum and turned away from them, feeling surrounded and stupid for how nervous the three of them were leaving him. Solas ran ahead but veered to the left, as if heading for the truck.

The sound of feet on grass. Feum instinctively ducked and twisted.

It wasn't enough. The branch smacked him across the top of his head, knocking him to the ground. Feum rolled onto his back, his sunglasses gone, the sun in his eyes, on his face. Panic gripped him and he scrabbled onto his side, attempting to get to his feet, to get to his house. To safety.

'You should have let us play with him. We are these woods,' said the boy, his tone harsh. Feum thought he could hear the creak of ancient trees in his voice, the sound of animals being born and dying while the forest looked on.

He had no words to reply. He got to his knees but before he could stand, the boy landed another blow. Feum sprawled back to the ground, covering his head and trying to protect himself. His hat was gone and the last blow made breathing difficult.

Solas was barking, running around Feum as he lay there waiting for the next one.

Instead he felt hands on his arms. Someone pulling at his gloves.

He wriggled free and threw them off. It was the

youngest of the three. 'I want to see what happens,' they said, as if he was doing something wrong by trying to protect himself.

'Let them take off your gloves,' said the girl. Her face was blank, as if she was wearing skin but not made of it.

'What's wrong with you?' he asked.

The boy stood over him, branch raised over his head. 'Let. Them. See. What. Happens,' he said and brought the branch down on Feum's chest. A bloom of lime scent made his eyes water.

He curled up into a ball. Outside of his world he heard the girl talking to Solas. 'We don't want to hurt him, but he was mean to us. We were here before him, this is our territory. You're in our pack now.' The dog stopped barking, was suddenly nosing Feum's face trying to get in. He wrapped his hands around Solas' head and held him close, but after a moment the dog withdrew.

Someone tugged at his shoes. They came off like he'd been shucked out of them. His socks were pulled free.

The sun continued to shine down and Feum started to burn.

'Please,' he said. 'I'm sorry.'

None of them answered him. Slowly but surely they took the rest of his clothes until he was naked. Each time he struggled or tried to stop them, the boy hit him. He felt bones break in his legs, in his arms. Feum covered his face trying to work out what was happening but rendered incapable by the pain.

After a while small fingers pried at his, tried to pull his broken hands away from where they still just about protected him.

'Just take the dog,' he said eventually through the gaps between his fingers. 'I'm sorry, please. Take him.'

The fingers came away, stopped trying to expose his face.

'See, Sunshine. He doesn't love you. He's not your pack.'

Solas whined, but Feum couldn't see him.

The sounds of the children and his dog faded.

A long time after they'd gone, Feum tried to move. His body was a rash of blisters and pus, of pain and fire, and no night was coming to ease his pain. He lay there and felt the thread of something crawling over his skin. He shivered, trying to get rid of it, but the sensation continued, wet, slimy, moving inexorably across his body. Eventually he opened his eyes and saw creepers slowly making their way across his seared skin, probing, testing where he was broken. With a sob he saw how they slowly pushed into his wounds as if he were a bag of fertiliser. Around him the trees had come back, had closed the clearing until only he was still in sunshine. They looked on at his broken form, woven now into the ground. He let out a sigh.

The sun would watch him, would burn him through the long midsummer night, and only the forest would see.

Midsummer Eve

Rachel Knightley

He was young. That was the first thing you noticed about that face. Not how pedantically symmetrical his features, not that his eyes were a strange, piercing hazel, or the way his hair parted exactly equally though he'd been lying on his side for so long. Not even the fact that he was dead. It was the sheer youth of him that stopped time.

It seemed an age before I dropped the hand. Either movement froze, or my mind's playback did. The hand gave a light bounce as it landed back in the long grass, snow-white on vivid green. 'How long do you think he's been here?' was all I said. There was no need to ask the bigger question: his eyes were too cloudy, fixed on distance as if searching for the right word, though horizontal between dew and mud. I'd never seen such stillness.

Nat shrugged. The familiar half-smile as he knelt opposite me between path and pond seemed cold, cruel even. It had to be shock. Nat's smile was always packed so full of enthusiasm he couldn't turn it off. Or if not shock, then denial: the mind's best gift to itself for surviving the short-term, facing the immediate. What I would not believe was this could be exactly what it looked like: thrill, that the worst had happened and to someone else. I would not believe that of Nat. 'Your phone or mine?' He stood up, palm spread in answer to his own question, head blocking out the sun.

I glared up into his bright halo, gave him my iPhone, and looked back at the body. It felt disrespectful to look away. My eyes recorded the bottle-green puffer jacket, black, unfashionably loose-legged Levi's, ruby Converse trainers, as if there'd be an exam on this boy, as if I could understand him back to life. But the smile that looked so inappropriate on Nat was itching onto the corners of my face. It was Nat's voice my thoughts tracked, rising and falling as his walk mapped the twists and turns of the narrow roads the emergency services would have to take from the main road to our corner of the common. "Your hand's so cold," I'd whispered to him only minutes before, along the edge of his ear.

"What?" Nat had whispered back, between gasps, between kisses so close to what I'd spent our three-year friendship imagining they'd felt perfectly natural.

"So cold," I'd repeated.

"But you aren't..." The words on his lips were hot and urgent breaths on mine.

"What?"

"You aren't..." He'd pulled back, face coming back into focus.

"What?"

"You aren't holding my hand."

And together we'd looked down at the hand mine had found in the long grass. I rubbed my own together now, still feeling the ghost of its solidity, the trace and chill of where it had been as if it were still there.

'No, there's no one else.' Nat was still circling, halfway across the field. The directions were done; these circles were his own now. There was something unconvincing in his absolute focus on the phone, showing us – me and the dead boy – his unconcern.

The dead boy had – ultimate past tense – the kind of face that would have still been boyish when he'd hit forty. His hair was almost exactly my own colour, but wavy brown instead of unimaginatively straight. While I'd had stubble since I was twelve, this boy – the lanyard around his neck claimed him as one of our own, though a different college – looked like he'd barely got that far even now. A decent figure, but too much muscle and not enough fat, suggesting all work and no play. What exercise he was giving his body was not about health but control. Perhaps I could have pointed out a happier path, had we been in time to meet on it.

'Alright. Yes. Yes, we'll be here.' Nat hung up, trotted back.

'Exercise addict,' I said, slipping the conversation into neutral.

'There are worse kinds.' He sat beside me, idly pulling up handfuls of grass. 'Anything else?'

There'd been no pain, I was sure of that. The boy had not seen death coming. He was distracted only by his own thoughts that were to remain frozen, unacted on. 'Nice face,' I said.

The silence continued long enough for me to notice it, and to look up into Nat's eyes. That half-smile of competition, that look away. Was he jealous of the boy at my feet, who had been sharing the silence with me? Probably not. I wouldn't credit him with that. For all his social success, it was lack of doubt, and with it lack of thought, not the ability to navigate them, that made Nat what he was. Even in death this boy had been thinking more than Nat ever did about anything. Why couldn't I have fallen for someone thoughtful, aware, someone who doubted themselves as much as I did? 'I know him,' Nat said, still looking out at the pond.

My skin went cold beneath the afternoon sun. 'What?'

'Alright. Knew.' He'd turned away but there was enough of his face to see the in-joke he was forming with himself. Trying to make me jealous of a corpse.

Knowing this, still I walked right in. 'You knew him? Who is he?'

'Does it matter?'

'You brought others here. Did you come here with him? Did he come here for you?'

'It's Olly,' he said.

'What?'

'Olly. Oliver Thornycroft. Gordon College.'

The lanyard around the dead boy's neck was blue, Gordon's colour. Nat wouldn't have seen that from his angle. 'You brought him here? Like you brought me here?'

'To talk? Yes.' He threw a stone at the water, ignored the effortless series of bounces before it disappeared. 'Doesn't matter now, does it.'

I looked back into that dead face with less trust now;

his silence was a betrayal of me, a mockery, where before I'd felt only sympathy and friendship. He'd been here first, in more ways than this. He was beyond jealousy; I could not follow where his eyes were looking. I shivered not at the certainty of death but at the delicate and tender way I'd tried to warm it. 'You told the police no one else was here.'

'What?'

'You denied my existence.'

'That wasn't it at all.'

'"We'll be here", you said. They thought you meant you and... Olly.'

'I meant you and me. Us.'

Even with my fingers clasped I felt my skin tingle at *Us*.

'You and me. That's what I meant. So did they.'

I tried more silence, then threw another stone at the pond. But my stone was heavier than his had been and failed to bounce a single time before it fell through the algae with a single plop. The rings hadn't dissipated before I gave up and snapped at him again. 'You're pretending nothing's happened.'

Nat was better at silence. Like all effortlessly popular people, he could under-think anything he didn't want to face. Even I'd forgotten what I been talking about by the time he finally said, 'Are you scared?'

'Of him? No.'

'You keep staring into his eyes. Losing yourself. I might get jealous.'

'I'm not expecting him to move.' Besides, it wasn't the eyes of death I feared. It was safer looking in Olly's eyes than Nat's. Neither would quite meet mine, but I had less to lose with Olly. And I wanted to be his friend. Even if the only thing I was in time for was to wait for the police to collect his body. Even if in life he'd been Nat's first choice over me. I wanted, though I knew he was gone, to be his friend. And it was the least we could do, wasn't it? With no way to help him, wasn't the least we could do to acknowledge him as long as possible?

'Don't believe in ghosts, then?'

'Of course not.'

He sat back on his haunches, looking over Olly at the pond. 'I suppose it was being back on that path, the one I had to come along to meet you here, made me think of it.'

'What?'

'The head.'

'What head?'

'You must remember the head? The disembodied head they found on the common. You did know?'

'Maybe.' There'd been some talk of it, but Nat's first year had been my gap year. I'd arrived old, quiet and at a disadvantage. The term "mature student" had a lot to answer for. Nat was twenty-one now, exactly the age one should be just after graduation. If mature meant confident – and as someone who'd prefer not to speak at all, I thought it did – he was more mature than I have any hope of ever being. I'd had more to be afraid of than what was beyond hurting me, or anyone. It was strange to think Nat could fear it – in the first place, let alone still fear it now.

'My idea of hell,' said Nat conversationally, 'is that

moment of creeping realisation that the path is never going to end. That you're always going to be alone on a path that, however familiar, you don't know how to get off.' The half-smile was fading, a new focus in his eye, looking inside at a world that was beyond him, rather than outside at the one he navigated so effortlessly. The flickering possibility of uncertainty, of fear. I tried not to stare. 'The one from uni towards the station is bright enough, God knows. That grassy bank stretching up one side where the main road forked away from the station. You can even see the edge of the platform, can't you?'

'Yes?' I'd never thought about the path. I'd just walked it.

'And today was midsummer, for God's sake. Midsummer, in the place I'd fallen for as soon as I stepped off the train! Knew was mine before I'd seen the university or anyone in it!' Another handful of grass and soil, then another. 'But there was always something about those trees on the other side. Something you didn't look in the eye.'

'Oh.' The path, for me, had led only to him. Especially today. There'd been a burst of sun on the sharp turn away from the platform, when the world disappeared in a shock of white. For my moment of half-blindness Nat had been little more than a fiery silhouette, a stick-man on fire. Then a dusting of cloud covered the sun and Nat seemed to feel my gaze, turning as soon as I truly saw him. When I raised a hand to my eyes, it was more in protection than greeting; his fair skin, bright eyes, the traces of a smile thin but strong, a smile that wanted to be bigger than the space allowed. His hands, clasped behind his back, were now clasped ahead of him, gold signet ring wiggling and igniting lashes of sunlight and reflected in a gentle shiver on his gold-brown hair. As he began walking, something had made me look away, dwell on the branches I was emerging from, watch the orange light dripping from the edges of the leaves. There was a quality to the sun on the grass, as I waited for him to reach me, so serene and solid and beautiful it made you certain someone would try and take it away. As if I'd known we were about to find Olly. As if finding Olly had always been inevitable.

'It wasn't even there they found it,' Nat continued, light as ever. 'They found the head – and an arm, or possibly two, I definitely remembered talk of separate bags – the other side of the wood.'

'And that's why you don't look at the trees?'

He shrugged and nodded at the same time, without losing that smile. 'It was freshers' week. You don't forget a first impression like that.' Then he was looking into Olly's eyes again.

Nat never made allusion to my copious silences; I didn't allude to his now. When mine came, far from the wall they seemed to appear as for others, Nat smiled right through it. Perhaps if only I could see it, I let myself think sometimes, that meant it wasn't real? Nat's smile dared me to think so. 'I don't think Olly was murdered,' I said. 'I don't think you do either.'

Nat sighed, the smile held. 'He'd mentioned heart trouble. But that sounded so dramatic. Something that would have had a fanfare, a final act. You would have seen it coming, not just...' He looked down, properly, for the first time, at Olly's eyes. 'Slipped away.' His brow furrowed, and he leaned closer. For a moment I thought he actually might turn, to see if he could see where Olly was looking. 'Still.' He looked up, and back at me with apparent satisfaction.

'Still.' The quality and colour of the leaves were too clear, too vivid. I had never felt so present, so alive. The common stretched out around us, green and gold, a silent, screaming call to action I had no idea how to accept.

He looked at me, and away again. 'It's the ghosts we fight so hard to keep here,' Nat said. 'They're the ones you have to watch.'

'What ghosts?'

'I see them everywhere, now we'll be leaving. Don't you? All over the common, the university. More of them all the time. The things that aren't going to happen if they haven't happened by now. The things you haven't said. Haven't done. The places they didn't happen.'

I looked away from Olly's eyes, almost as far as Nat's.

'I mean...' He shook his head. 'Look at it.'

'At what?'

He looked at me like he couldn't believe I was asking. The grass stretched out, green and flat and wide, as far as we could see, as if we were its intended centre. Eventually it was fenced by trees, and the purr of the main road beyond them, but wide enough to feel limitless. At least, limitless from where we sat.

'Days like this are treacherous,' he said, destroying more of the grass as if it were the common's fault. "They make you believe you really could hold the moment, grasp it it in your hand, understand it in some way that would prevent it from moving on. But we can't. You do realise that? As slowly as it's moving, this grass and our time on it is still being swept out from under our feet like a gigantic rug?'

I felt his eyes move down, just as mine did, from this vision of forever to its edge, where Olly lay. 'I know,' I said.

'How could you not?' Nat looked back over my shoulder, for a moment, at the distance it had seemed to me Olly was looking into. 'It's the way you start to see everything, every action and every person in the context of...' He looked away. 'Of how lucky you are to be there in the first place. Mortal fear is exactly like falling in love, isn't it? They both make you so sure you want to keep on living.' He touched a finger to my face, traced the bristly contour of my jaw. 'How did you get to be so young?'

'I'm four years older than you.'

'You're younger than I've ever been.' He looked at me across those four years into which he'd crammed so much life. We were still kissing when the police arrived.

'Well, I've certainly never had to break up a threesome like this.' I didn't recognise the amusement in the policewoman's voice at first. From the moment we jumped away from each other and up from the dead boy at our feet in a cloud of rapid and overlapping apology, we were more laughed at than told off. They didn't seem to take much time worrying we'd killed him. Her juniors – not much older than us – just smiled and looked away from us as Nat and I had from each other. Then they started putting the plastic tent up. Even before we stood at different corners of the field to give our statements, which must have matched because they said they'd get on better without us, the embarrassment floating around us was enough for anything else to melt away. All these decades gone and I still wonder if that wasn't the real lesson. 'So we can go?' was all I said – or thought – at the time.

The sergeant standing in front of the tent they'd erected over Olly looked at me in a surprisingly maternal way. I cannot see her clearly now. Though she probably wasn't more than thirty-five, at the time she was that mythical creature, a real adult: as far removed a creature from my own reality as a gryphon or a unicorn. 'That question suggests a level of patience we don't associate with undergraduates.'

'Graduates,' I corrected.

'Sorry?' She looked from Nat to me and back again.

'Adults. We graduated last week.'

She looked from him to me again. Under that gaze, I had never felt so young in my life. 'My mistake, sir.'

Nat took my hand, the bubbling of silent laughter coated in that all-consuming half-smile. We walked back down the path towards the university. The path he'd half-admitted to being afraid of shimmered with all the confidence of eternity, as any summer day always will. Perhaps it was the arrogance of knowing that, in one form or another, it would return and survive as not one of us passing through it would. Even if it was laughing at me, I couldn't help smiling with it.

These days, it's this bit I'm angry with myself for.

With Nat as far from me now as Olly was then, I can't help feeling even now there was something I could have done; some password that, had I only known, I could have fed into the day to make it do what it looked so ready to do: last forever. But as I slip back now towards that memory, I don't entirely mind that I failed.

Midsummer Eve

Linda Nagle

He constructed me on a whim and constricts me via verse and structure, all the while introducing character and conflict – and signifying nothing. Certain aspects are left to my design, I will give him that, although he has made it known that there is special providence in the fall of a sparrow: many acts have been written for me since my days as a mewling baby – and I must admit to having performed them to mixed reviews. With quill and prescription, he has made sure to present me with all manner of imagery, odd props, and relentless dramatics to adorn the prefabricated stage of my existence – although it should be known that on more than one occasion, I have had cause to make myself another face.

One June, in my scenes as an unbruised youth, I crept – as a snail – to a fortune teller's tent, hoping for some narrative assistance. Me, a poor player with decades in front and little between the ears; I was a vixen when I went to school, instead favouring Mother Nature as my teacher.

Madame Portia professed to see tomorrows in the garden of my palm; as a constant gardener, she sowed the seeds of time there and could say which grains would grow and which would not. Her tent of red a theatrical backdrop on the forest's florid stage, this local habitation was the perfect beckoning-place for the hitherto unseen seer to manipulate her prey. The festival itself a good welcome for a merry feast, her inviting canvas walls extended warm displays in the common tradition, form, and ceremonious duty: *Astounding! Incredible! A direct link with the deceased!* I didn't believe a word of it, of course, but as a teen, I did have a taste for something wicked.

Before it would come my way, though, I should have to pause – upon a bank of violets, the line for divination to the so-called spiritual plane extended past three other tents, and I did not fancy joining it. Instead, I settled on the lush, lusty grass outside the teller's temporary home and listened intently to wound and poultice through the well-travelled fabric; I would await my cue and approach the prophet once age and complaint were over, and as soon as fermentation – that familiar old creature – had had its way with the bawdier players. Beer tents tendering liquid dishes for kings, the queue for the newest prophecy was about to find itself contending with one of the oldest pills: a sniff of wine here, a quart of ale there, and the poorest, unhappy brains would be bound to drink themselves away.

Please do not misunderstand – I am neither the drinking kind nor entirely virtuous; I am perfectly able to appreciate the appeal of strong concoctions, for it can be a tonic to drink down all unkindness. But to have my own performance continue, abstinence had become necessary, along with the acknowledgement – even at fifteen – that the best safety lies in fear. At that age, a year before my encounter with Madame Portia, I had already pledged to touch the stuff no longer, since the cheapest cider had provoked a pair of boys to hang on me, their rising appetite increasing further as it fed on the void left by the disappearance of my consent. My scribe had given my mind permission to lose itself to a brewed stupor; to sleep, perchance to lose consciousness completely. There is no virtue like necessity: vowing never again to put myself in the position where I must choose between a pot of ale and safety, I invented some other customs of entertainment. And, back in the forest, customs proved plentiful: I considered (and quickly dismissed) the equally unhealthy habit of tobacco-taking, eventually settling upon the hobby of logic in the hope of contradicting the seer with impeccable argument. But for one who spoke an infinite deal of nothing, even the cynic in me could not dispute that she had passion and persuasion in her song.

For in my greenest home amongst the trees – where temperance and patience had me wait – I heard her speak in rhythm with such ease, so confident was she in paid debate. She spoke in beats of ten – as five-by-two – a song her paying customers believed; odd prophecies were spoken as if true; new comforts offered hope for the bereaved.

After she had laid down the circumstances for imaginings and payment, I heard the soothsayer treat kindly those of crabbed age: the petulant oldsters whose chemical and churchlike ways worked both for and against them, their lives but walking shadows. Big with rich increase, autumnal people are likely to plummet the farthest, I found: colouring themselves silly with bitter babble and infernal chatter – chatter that spews forth like a relentless rainbow daubed across a sky they do not bother to see; all they care about is the rain that falls from it, or what the sun can do for them. Will it colour their skin? Shall they be able to hang out their linen? And whilst our sun never changes, shining brightness perpetual, there are those who choose never to see the light, despite the turning of the earth.

I learned this as an observer both at home and out in the woodland: only and always the selfishness and the gossip, only and always naught but foul whisperings concerning the youth of today. I did not much mind that I was amongst the young number in question.

Soon after the aged, the broken had their turn. The shattered of spirit or of body, with their afflictions and sticks, and those either blinded by love or as blind as it, who looked instead with the mind and saw only precious treasure. Disease and dis-ease aside, those were the folk who hoped for the most, because they *hoped* the most. They dared dream. They were wont to allow into their imaginings all manner of belief and wonder – I could see it in their tears, their smiles, and imagined it underneath their clothes as they left the tent – underneath their skin, even, swimming through their veins, popping. Popping and pulsing. Pulsing and coursing for a charm of powerful trouble.

A break, then, while I heard the old woman pour and sip and swallow. And a fight, next, full of sound and fury: bearded debauchers at war, filled with the strangest oaths. A thirst for sleep and urination had they, and they were quick in quarrel. With their collective histories condensed into one predictable volume, their predetermined actions inevitable, little time seemed to pass before they began to tire of the queue and headed immediately for another, desperate for the mirth and merriment that only liquid sustenance could offer.

Soon, news came down the line that one of the drinkers had looked his last, passing suddenly to the gloomy shade right there in the bloody mud, flat on his face in a beer-soaked splat. I crept towards the scene, which was well-lit and rich with character, but I could barely get past the crowd. In his hair, they told, a headband of tiny yellow daffodils, cushioning his head – a pretty pillow for his passage into the ground whence he came (although whispers quickly passed from person-to-person that he had dropped there swift as a shadow – out of nowhere and without notice). A healthy (ha!) splash of the reddest wine was said to have marked his beige uniform, so I took solace in the likelihood he had left this plane sated and happy. I did smile, though, at the idea of a man meeting his maker in such a state, for while I did not believe in religion, I could easily envisage an audience lapping up the scene from this, one of the finest comedies of error.

I put all thoughts of the drinker aside and returned to my mark, escaping the babbling crowd. All the devils were here; writing sorrow on the bosom of the earth seemed to be the order of the day. Each category – every persuasion – added up to little more than drivel and dirge, conveying outline and caricature but signifying nothing. Such are the sad mathematics of people, and such are the ways of life. People: hazy, forsaken toys whose static unforgiveness and unbendable ways fester desensitised, nonsensical unethics. Life waits for them to wail, to mould their own forms into the scabbed shapes of death, and soils their character ere they be dirtied down by whatever feverish habit pleases them the most. And through it all, all sorts of simple people have kept a complicated faith: in horrible monsters and odd gods and omens, and in prophecies, dreams, and magic, for they consider that believing in heaven makes them heavenly. For them, the ominous must be established that horror might be averted. I could not comprehend how it was that they reached their conclusions – how they were ever able to determine which auguries should be considered genuine – and I remained especially baffled by howsoever they dealt with their demons whenever hell found itself empty.

No, not for me black cats and ladders, although life, it is said, has supposedly been – and shall always be – foreseen. But I disbelieved it then, and I disbelieve it now. Any faith I have is kept plain and simple. Mediums, media ... no such thing. Palm-crossers are the diddled, fortune tellers the rippers-off. I kept that in mind as I anticipated my scene, certain that the old woman should smell my cynicism across a boundless sea – I was but one drop of blood in an ocean of sharks.

❖

2

I already had her as a dishonourable liar, and she should be certain on first glance to take me for a doubter, only there for the fun and the sorrow of it. Jesters do oft prove prophets, though, so I vowed to keep my honour bright, and persevere.

'These rules be mine, preventing cause for doubt: into my palm place golden coins ten; or folded notes that spell the same amount – more payment if I must begin again.'

Her eyes a very unsettling blue, I immediately spotted behind them the potential for cankerous rancour were I to cross her. I forced my pride down my throat and paid the woman with some of my father's money, a pinch of salt at the ready.

'I see a boy – a man – of great import; the letter J be featured in his name;

''Tis Jacob... Jake... which man do I report? Ah, Jeremy, no – Joshua, no – James?'

What's in a name? She could have said anything. She might have selected any letter. Odds and degrees of separation being what they are, it is not unreasonable of me to suggest that clairvoyants do indeed see people coming. Both reasoned and random selections have an equal chance of hitting home: everybody knows a person or two who once had a cousin or a brother with an 'e' in their name, or who once lived in Stockholm, or who might attribute significance to the number seven. But, for the common comfort that it caused, I allowed her to continue.

‘’Tis Julian – or Jonathan, perhaps; forgive me, do, this momentary lapse.’

After listing seemingly as many as forty thousand brothers, she all but gave up on the favoured initial, eventually imparting that I’d be betrothed before the month was out (even though those married young are often unhappy), and gifting me the precise date I should start to look upon my way to dusty death. A man would fall into my lap, I must look out for life repeating itself, and I should deem important any images that chose to display themselves. All tragic tomorrow-and-tomorrow-and-tomorrow words signifying nothing – and told by an idiot.

‘Before you go, dear Juliet,’ she said, ‘You should know this: a time will come to leave; pray do not ’come confused ’twixt love and bed; trust only hearts that rest upon the sleeve.’

Now there they were – new words to comprehend. She spoke once more, of violent delights, and how such ways must offer violent ends; this news, to me, caused something of a fright. For future antidote, she had no balm: ‘a remedy inside yourself’, she spoke. And as she walked me out, she took my arm: ‘Have children three, then play your masterstroke.’

By the old woman’s reckoning, I’d have several summers to fathom what she meant – if her words had meant anything at all, of course, and if my author were to will it so.

❖

3

Ever since their union, and full of the milk of human kindness, my mother had excused and mollycoddled the decrepit character of my father, who took delight in displeasure and chose misery over contentment. I had entered stage left in the ninth year of their union, joining a pair of brothers who, at the time of my birth, already made a combined age of fourteen. And as my plot developed, so did my senses: this was a tragedy in the making. I heard it so – and I could smell it. It was there in the low tones and bragging horror of my father's voice. But I had neither learned my lines nor had them read to me; I was blind back then to the truth and the fear of it. That it was written for me to see out at least four decades – before I must speak the things I felt – would be lost on me until the scene in question were to play out. Unaware that I was bound, one day, to heave my heart into my mouth, and that my mother would – ultimately – follow my lead, the institution would carry on doing its damage throughout my formative years.

The sounds from the next bedroom – more than a pretty folly – would wave and weave their way through walls of paper until they reached my midnight ears. Not for my parents the pleasures of marriage, but one-sided fights and maternal tears coating shattered orbs of fragile glass, the violence of grief foisting itself onto and into my mother's heart, with pressure produced and directed by my father. Stumbling on his abuse, I was ashamed to be his child.

He projected his own shame, too, all the way to the back of the auditorium: with my having sinned at fifteen he had made sure to convince me it had all been my fault. Had I not taken a drink, I would not have been in the position of permitting such an uprising. Had I selected a wardrobe more pious in origin, those boys might not have looked twice. And were my young face to have refrained from tribal war-paint, as he called it, he would have had no cause for painting his only daughter as a nymphomaniac. Those were his words, and he spoke them badly, although I heeded them well and drank back every last one successfully, filling up the shameful tank of self-blame I stored within. I would do well, he said, to have Satan for a playmate.

At sixteen, I had visited a fortune-teller with the aim of debunking my father's spiritual notions and disproving the existence of his god – so impossibly complicated was my father's character to invent that surely no author had he. Madame had pressed upon me the importance of leaving, but I was unable to ascribe any significance to her song until I had taken on the military role of mother, fighting the greatest battle of my life, and choosing between ale and safety.

4

I proved the seer wrong, marrying at the relatively old age of thirty-one. A strange oath was had, where we pledged ourselves to the other as we were then, not how we would be. I must have been a terrible wife, too, for although I regarded my husband with the entire contents of my heart, I find it difficult now to accept that he so much as liked me – even a little. I would annoy him with my existence and via word and song – he would tell me off for the pauses I would leave, mid-sentence, whilst considering carefully the message I was attempting to convey, and when I would sing, the tunes must have been so off-key that he would make other noises to drown me out. This was clearly not the food of love, but on I played.

Brim-filled with bad habits and irksome ways was I that he soon let his preferences be known, ultimately spending his nights with bottle and glass, instead. I suppose I had driven him to it, for, in his words, 'what else was there?' What else was there, indeed, if I would not share a drink with him?

His nightly escape into his world of inebriation must have served the man some comfort away from his terrible wife – a description befitting my character, I felt. I knew how dreadful he considered me, for he was sure to point out just how misguided my love and how incorrect my habits. With an eventual trio of little ones, I considered it wise to remain just as abstinent an adult as I had been a youth, lest emergency dictate common sense and journey. This was a particular virtue of mine, one from which I refused deviation; I felt it imperative that at least one parent should always remain in control of their faculties. But again, this may have been an error in my judgement – I knew this because he would tell me so. He would tell me how mistaken my sentiment and how irregular my behaviour. 'Every normal person drinks a glass before bed. Most people share a bottle of wine a night – you are the odd one out.'

However many times he attempted to persuade me to enter his world, I kept about me my sanity and my wits – not in preparation for battle, but for my children. I would have to remain, as he put it, 'in the wrong.' And although I would cry about his argument and beat myself up over his tone, he never once laid a hand on me. Part of me wished that he had done so, for then I would have had visible proof of his nature, although I did not, at the time, recognise the traits so obviously cut from the same fabric as my father. I would be at fault for every argument; my husband would explain his anger away by declaring it a reaction to my behaviour, for I was written as all women are. This is not to say that I did not analyse the beginnings of us, with a view to establishing the obvious plot-holes that had been present since act one of our union. Perhaps the signs were there, or perhaps the imagery signified nothing.

Sighing and fawning, I had had him instantly as the father of the three children I would bear. Hooked into the same trap as many other female characters before me, by a man who said all the right things; rather, *the wrong* things, but in the right-sounding way to deceitful ears. He spoke of my beauty as if it were an achievement, one that would bestow a trophy upon him. I drank it all in as he spoke of his lost love and the abuse he had suffered at her hand. She had had the gall – the sheer audacity – to call the authorities for help, when she had been the perpetrator all along, and he had been asked to leave his own home. Back then, I was delirious as his new love, happy to be ensnared with his harmful charm and happier still to have an enemy in his former partner. She was the one to beat. She was the one to surpass. But I plainly failed to realise he was telling me all along who he was, and I was refusing to listen – just as I had refused to listen to the seer at sixteen.

Choosing not to see the person he was showing me, I concentrated on his good side instead. His constant gardening had our plants flourishing (he was very attentive towards flora if not to me) and the balloons I had kept from the early days would stay inflated for at least half a dozen years.

And that romance, that early romance, was good. In the beginning, I saw that it was good. He would play with words and invent silly plurals to have me laugh, appreciating my love of words. He would quote my favourite songs: although he hadn't been looking, somehow he had found me. It would later transpire, of course, that this was all part of the trap along with the beautiful garden. The narcissus had always been his favourite flower and yet the irony was completely lost on me.

Act two began with our first child – and a gestation that did not go particularly well, for I was taken ill throughout and filled myself with additional worry. Who would get me to a midwife? I was unable to transport myself in that state, and he refused to put down the bottle, even during the final trimester. But I showed too much concern, he told me. 'It's fine – we can ask my father. He will take us.'

I did not consider it too much to expect temporary sobriety from my husband, or that he would want to be the one to take his wife to birth his child, but perhaps that deluded expectation was another of my annoying habits that caused his hatred of me. In the end, he chose an existence without me and with the fruits of the vine, heating his liver with it and thus further cooling his heart.

For the longest time, I learned tolerance of his manifestations, and would creep downstairs to make sure that while he was passed out, he could still breathe. I would ensure he stayed warm, and kept a blanket down there for that purpose. None of it was enough to have him love me, though – or even have him wish to spend time with me, but as I have said, I must have been a terrible wife. I did not fully embrace his love of nature, for one. Despite my scepticism, some of his more pagan leanings were harmless, and might even have been endearing were it not for the liquid poison running through the veins of our marriage. He would enjoy Beltane and midsummer and build statues of wicker twigs to be burned in the garden as an offering to his favourite story, and I ignored it all. I did not fully appreciate the weeks we had spent together in Padstow and all the other Cornish towns, where festival and revelry provided the perfect floral backdrops to a softer, more easily-watchable drama. Had I done so, had I better-embraced his sober ways, the intoxicated ones might not have developed as dramatically. Or am I second, third, fourth-guessing myself? I cannot name that which was bound to happen, nor can I lay claim to intervention.

All flowers may as well have been torn from the garden as the arc of his character hit a devastating peak in act three: he lost all music in himself and began to actively hurt the children. He would hold our son's mouth closed whenever he was too loud for tolerance, and fell down, drunk, while carrying one of our daughters. I accepted finally, then, that our ending was in sight, unable to stand by and watch him destroy himself and take our beautiful children with him wherever he was going. I loved him until the end, but I loved the little ones more.

I knew I must force love – and myself – to look with the eyes for once, and eventually found strength in the arms of another, who wanted me and loved me – nay, adored me – just the way I was. I had neither sought a new friend nor the company of a stranger, but I had never been more full: full of requited love and promise.

He died there and then, as he would do a thousand times before his death. The moment I announced the end of our union, I saw the life leave his eyes that a demon might enter – and enter, it did. A side of him revealed itself that I had never before witnessed, although the seeds had been sown at the start. All the signs had been evident, and had I opened my eyes and my heart, I would have noticed them, so I began to consider parts of the seer's prophecy accurate: I had found the remedy precisely where she had directed.

I knew he would recover well, if not from the drinking then from my betrayal and from my terrible performance as a wife. He had already established the outline of his story and would rewrite it with a new love, ensnaring her with the self-same hooks he had used on me. The repeated imagery was all set up for him in readiness of a remake: she had my face; she even had my name. And to her, I was the new antagonist.

5

I have performed my own prologue for some time now, and have written many different conclusions to my story. Of course, I have had to run every word past my author, who remains in the background as always, the wings being his preferred habitat. Whether my life has always been written this way, or whether I have played some part in my own outcomes (or those of others) is not for me to say. But when the father of my children was found dead at a midsummer festival this year, face-down in a puddle of bloody mud, I had cause to question my sanity. It is said that he dropped there out of nowhere and without notice, swift as a shadow. A sixteen-year-old girl was found underneath him, in the grasses beside a fortune-teller's tent, equally as dead as he.

But I am sure that this signifies nothing. Yes – this signifies nothing.

Midsummer Eve

Robert Shearman

That summer fling I had with Eve Gershwin was not my most tender and by no means my most satisfying. But I suppose it was one of my most memorable, and isn't that often the way? Proper love, the stuff that makes you happy, that makes you get up in the morning with a spring in your step and a song in your heart, all that guff – it's nice to live through, but it rarely provides substance for a good anecdote. And whatever Eve was, and wherever she is now – because she took pains to put a lot of distance between us once our summer together was over – she was certainly an anecdote. Something to chat about over a beer with my mates. Even if that does make me feel a bit guilty. It seems disrespectful. Because there was passion, wasn't there? Not love, I mean, definitely not love – but *something,* surely. I suppose there has to have been.

Many friends warned me about dating Eve Gershwin, and, to be fair, none of them more openly or accurately than Eve Gershwin herself. "I give my heart away too easily," she said over dinner, "and maybe that's why I take it back again so often." She speared a prawn with her fork, put it in her mouth, and chewed – chewed, I thought, for rather longer than the prawn warranted. "I'm fickle," she concluded, and shrugged, and smiled.

And I suppose I asked her out as an act of hubris, I thought that I could be the one to tame her. She was, I think you'll know this already, alarmingly attractive. Alarming, as in the sense that when you saw her, it made you wonder why you'd wasted your time with so many plainer girls beforehand – no one wants to have to question their whole romantic past like that, and in all the time that I knew her I don't think I ever saw a man look entirely *happy* in her presence. Excited, sometimes, certainly. With one or two of the older men, even surprised and grateful. But she wasn't a woman who inspired joy on any level. Joy simply wasn't what Eve Gershwin was about.

When I first met Eve, I'd been going out with Alice for quite a while. We were coming up to celebrating our six month anniversary – by which I mean, the six month milestone was all Alice was talking about, and how we should mark the occasion, how much the presents we should give each other should cost, and whether we should throw a party. In retrospect I find all the faff about an anniversary that wasn't even an anniversary rather endearing, but at the time it really got on my wick. So I was probably already pissed off with Alice when I saw Eve that day standing by the photocopier trying to correct a paper jam. She wasn't glammed up or anything, she was by a photocopier, for Christ's sake, but there was a beauty to her that seemed quite natural and unforced and clear. – Alice wasn't beautiful. Alice wasn't ugly, but she wasn't beautiful. Alice wouldn't have looked good, all hot and irritated by a hunk of malfunctioning office hardware. And I didn't break up with Alice straight away, it wasn't as simple as that, it wasn't one look at Eve and, you know, bang, my whole life had changed. – But, that said, I'd got rid of Alice within the week.

Nor did I make a move on Eve straight after. She was new to the office, and that meant she'd be the pickings of upper management first. Besides, there was no good reason why she would want to go out with me. I'm not a looker, I know that – not ugly either, but very definitely in Alice's league. When Alice and I had photos taken you could see that we sort of fitted together in them, we were of the same species, she had about as much wrong with her as I had wrong with me. Indeed, that *helped*, her buck teeth were offset by my fat jowels, and vice versa, we were complementarily plain.

Beside Eve there was nothing complementary about it. But I asked her out for two reasons. One was that I'd had a very slight promotion. Nothing to change my job title or the size of my office cubicle, but there was a bit of extra money coming in, and bags more responsibility – and my ego felt good and inflated and *bold*. And the other reason, I knew Eve was single. She'd been going out with Greg from the human resources team, but that was all over now, I didn't know Greg but I heard he was quite cut up about it. I made my play. And I did it so confidently that I wasn't even surprised when she said yes. It wasn't until I got home that evening that my legs began to wobble and the doubt set in.

But the date went well. I'll say one thing for Eve

Gershwin, she gives good dates. She'd dressed up really nicely, it made me feel flattered to have something so classy by my side, and even the waiters looked impressed – at one point she went to powder her nose, and I was able to look around the entire restaurant and see that every man in the place was looking at me with frank admiration. And we talked easily, and the conversations overlapped, but never in an annoying way, only because there seemed so much to say. Though I suppose it's true I can't remember now one thing we actually talked about. Still, we were still at it after the dessert and the coffee, and I asked Eve if I could see her safely home, and she said that would be nice. And I helped her with her coat, I even offered her my arm – sort of jokey, you know, so there'd be nothing wrong if she rejected it – but she didn't reject it, she took my arm in hers as if that was what we *always* did, as if this wasn't our first date but our hundredth, and as we walked out on to the street I imagined all the restaurant applauding me.

The summer evening was pleasantly warm, and we stayed arm in arm all the way to her house, which slowed us down somewhat; we still got to her house far too soon. I had to cut short one of my anecdotes, and I was telling it better than I had ever told it before, it seemed not only amusing but had depth and point. "Well," she said, "this is me." "Well," I said. I wondered if she'd invite me in. She didn't. But that wasn't a surprise, we both had to be at the office in the morning. "Would you like to see me again?" I asked; she said, "I think you're going to be very special to me." And that was more than I'd bargained for, I thought, oy oy! I said, "How about we do it again this weekend?", and she smiled.

We kissed then. I put in a bit of effort, gave her one of Alice's favourites, the one with the tongue flick, we were kissing for at least three minutes. Until we got to the point where I thought she'd have to ask me in. Until I thought etiquette demanded it. "Well," she said, "well, good night." And she went indoors. And I didn't feel bad about that, I didn't, it was fine, it was better than fine, actually – and as I walked to the bus stop I was already trying to work out what I should get her for Christmas – six full months to go, but I'd made it to six months with Alice, why couldn't I with Eve? – and whether we should spend it with my parents or with hers, and actually I thought we'd go to my parents, because it would be so much fun to show off a girlfriend like Eve to my family, especially after all the Alice lookalikes I'd brought home, oh, the look there'd be on my father's face, he'd always wanted a girl like Eve, and the best he'd ever got was my Mum. He'd be fucking drooling! – and if I could get her to glam up like she had on our date, it'd knock his fucking socks off.

At the office the next day Eve and I didn't talk, but there was nothing unusual in that. I smiled at her a couple of times, though, and she smiled back.

I was full of plans for Saturday night, and it didn't matter that I kept changing my mind what they'd be. We didn't have to do everything at once, we'd have lots and lots of Saturdays to fill, all the world would be our oyster and we would enjoy exploring every last bit of it.

On Friday night when she phoned me I think I'd got planned a movie and a curry. "Hello," she said. "Look, I think we'll have to cancel tomorrow night."

"Oh," I said. As her boyfriend, I did the good boyfriend thing, I immediately expressed concern for her health, and kept the disappointment as far from my voice as possible.

"I'm perfectly well," she said. "I just think we should call it a day."

I was quite surprised by this. I asked her why. "Does everything have to have a reason?" she said. I asked her if we were now just going to be good friends, and I'm not sure that by this time the disappointment wasn't seeping in perfectly fucking audibly.

And she thought a bit. And then said, "Honestly, I'm not sure your friendship would mean that much to me."

And that was that.

I must stress, I wasn't upset by this. I wasn't. I hardly knew the girl. I was confused, that was all, and who can blame me? Had I behaved too coolly in the office towards her? But I had only been trying to act professional. I had seen the way some of her boyfriends had moved around her, as if trying to assert to the world that she was their property – Greg, for example, and that had been nauseating (and it hadn't done the tosser much good in the end, had it?). Was it the kiss? Because if it were the kiss, I could try again, I had a whole range of other kisses to choose from. I phoned her back, but she didn't answer, and I thought she was probably blocking my number. So I put on my coat and went out to ring her from the public phone box near the supermarket. Still no answer, maybe she'd gone out.

I wasn't upset. It was her loss. And it wasn't as if I'd sacrificed anything for Eve, no more than an evening of my time and the price of a three-course Italian meal. I hadn't broken up with Alice because of Eve. Alice and I had been on the way out anyway.

Before I went to bed, I tried phoning Eve one more time. Nothing. So I went to sleep.

And then I was upright.

It was the immediacy of it that disturbed me most, that first time. Not the absurdity of it – that I'd gone from a comfy horizontal position to one that was very definitely and uncompromisingly vertical. Nor the change of location, because I could see immediately I had moved – I had *moved*, for God's sake! – even in the dark I could see I had moved! I was still in a bedroom, but not in my own bedroom. This was a woman's bedroom, it was neater than mine, and there was the whiff of perfume, scented soap. I was standing up, straight as a ramrod, in a woman's bedroom, when I ought to have been lying down in mine – and that still wasn't it, that wasn't what set my heart racing, that wasn't what was making me start to freak out (take it easy!) – it was the sheer *speed* with which I'd ended up there, as if I'd been catapulted into position – catapulted, yes, that was the word for it – I felt all my limbs jangling with the rush of it all, and my hair out of place, and I tried to catch my breath but it was difficult, I had to suck the air in deep and pant it out, actually pant the thing, before I could feel myself calm down.

And my first impulse for all that new breath I'd earned was to waste it, was to cry out for help.

"Don't say a word," whispered a voice behind me.

So I didn't. I decided not to worry about the voice. The voice could take care of itself for now. Let me worry about the other things first.

I was standing over the sleeping body of Eve Gershwin. At least, I assumed she was sleeping – oh, God, what if she were dead? – oh, God, what if the police caught me in her bedroom and she were dead, how would I explain that? But then she gave a little snore, not so much a snore as a little sigh, it was rather sweet, really, and warm, and feminine – so, so she wasn't dead, that was good, so when the police stormed in I'd only have to explain why I was standing in her bedroom at all (oh yes, that would be *so* much better) – and I decided I had better get out of there as soon as possible. Before she stirred. Before she saw me.

And my feet wouldn't move.

And I thought, that was unhelpful of them – and I thought, maybe they were numb. Maybe numbness was some side effect of all that impossible catapulting my body had just been put through. Or even worse. Worse, paralysed, I'd be stuck like this forever! So I sent a message down to my toes to wiggle, and they wiggled in response quite amiably – my feet would do anything I wanted, they cheerfully informed me, except walk away from Eve Gershwin's bedside. I was meant to be here, and this is where they were going to keep me. Well, I wasn't going to put up with a rebellion like that. I bent down, I was going to pick the fuckers up by *hand*, I was going to carry myself out of the room by force if I had to! – and I couldn't find the feet amid the tangle of the white sheets I was wearing. And that's when I first realised I was wearing white sheets at all. I hadn't gone to bed at home wearing sheets; I'd gone to bed naked, actually, and thank God that wasn't still the case, that would make that explanation to the police that little bit more complicated. But sheets – I was all in white, a gleaming white, I bet I was lighting up the room with how I gleamed. There was a hole cut in the sheet for my head, there were no holes for the arms. I was dressed like a ghost. It wasn't a good costume. It would have shamed the seven-year-old trick or treaters who might have worn it at Halloween.

"Not at yourself," the voice hissed. "Look at *her*. Do the job you're here for."

So I looked.

I never had had the chance to study a woman quite so completely before. And especially not a beautiful one; my formative adolescent years had been spent gazing not at the pretty girls I knew would object, but at the dumpy ones who'd be lucky to care. As a result I had grown up acquainted only with the folds of flesh that gather around a woman's face, the flecks of dandruff, the patches of make-up used to mask spots and blackheads – a whole gamut of big arses and lopsided breasts and faces that just somehow looked a bit *wrong*. Real beauty was something airbrushed in lingerie advertisements and my elder brother's top-shelf mags. But I gazed down at Eve Gershwin, and here, indeed, was real beauty. On my date with her I'd stolen a few long glances at her face when she was chatting, but never for too long in case she noticed what I was doing. I'd had to look away at the menu, at the table, straight down at the floor. Now I could examine her without interruption.

In sleep Eve was so peaceful, only that sighing snore breaking through the still every now and then. A smile played about her face, she must have been dreaming about something very nice. Or even something rather naughty! – and even in the dark her lips were thick and red. Her hair was down and poured out over her chest, there was something liquid about it, it emphasised her breasts and the smooth milkiness of her neck – it looked quite artfully posed, but it couldn't have been, could it? – Oh, Alice had never looked good asleep. There'd be spittle. And some nights she'd thrash about as if she were trying to punch me out of bed.

It was easy watching Eve. If this were my job, as the voice said, it was hardly an unpleasant one. The time passed before I knew it. And then I felt a tap upon my shoulder. And instinctively I turned around, before I even remembered my feet were frozen and I couldn't move, and they were free, they had unglued themselves.

"It's my turn now," whispered a man. He too was dressed in a white sheet. I saw, to my surprise, it was old Mr Willis from the board of directors.

"Yes, sir," I said, and gave him my place – although I could feel straight after there was no need to defer, office politics were irrelevant here. We were all equal before the might of Eve Gershwin.

There wasn't just Mr Willis in the room. In the back, in the shadows, there must have been a dozen other ghosts. One of them waved at me, impatiently, to join them. When I got close I saw it was Greg from the Human Resources team.

"That's your shift done for the night," he whispered. "Two a.m., to two thirty. Watching over Eve, and protecting her from harm." I looked at Greg, and in the office he'd always struck me as a bit of a prick, someone who was more interested in talking about football and beer than in the productivity graphs he was supposed to. Here in Eve Gershwin's bedroom his face was deadly serious. And I looked at the other ghosts flanking him – some I recognised vaguely from the office, most I didn't – and their faces were just as hard-set and stern.

So when Greg smiled it wasn't a warm smile. "You did well," he said. "Well done."

I would rather have liked to have gone home then. But I wasn't able to leave the room. My hand wasn't able to grasp the doorknob properly, it was like syrup.

All the ghosts had to pay witness. We watched over each other as we watched over Eve.

It was, frankly, rather dull. I wished I'd brought my iPhone, or a book, maybe.

Old Mr Ellis wasn't content to watch. From his feet frozen position he was still able to bend forward over Eve. He would stroke her hair. He would kiss at his fingers, then wipe his fingers over her cheeks. He said to her things, so quietly that we couldn't hear.

"Is he allowed to do that?" I whispered to Greg.

"We can do what we want," Greg whispered back. "It's not as if we can wake her, no matter how hard we try."

"Then why on earth are we whispering?"

He looked at me coldly. "Out of respect."

I wondered how long all this would take. It would be dawn soon, and at least five ghosts hadn't had a turn yet.

"I think there's been some mistake," I said. "I shouldn't really be here."

"There's no mistake. Passion has brought you here."

And I wanted to point out that I'd only snogged her the once, and looking back it wasn't even one of my good snogs, I knew I could have done better. But the way Greg spoke was so solemn, sanctimonious even, like this was so serious, like we were in a *church* or something, I don't know. And the other ghosts all around looking serious too, as if the church service were a wedding, or a funeral, yes, more like a funeral, because there was no joy in it – and I saw how even off duty they were all still staring at Eve Gershwin's sleeping body, and with such rapt fascination, with such *love* – and I decided to keep my mouth shut.

Around five o'clock another ghost shuffled into position. He began prodding at Eve's breasts, then cupping them, weighing them like fruit. He made strange little grunting noises.

"Come on!" I said. "How is that protecting her?" But no one answered.

"This isn't going to keep happening, is it?" I asked eventually. "Not night after night? How do I get it to stop?" And the ghosts were scandalised. This wasn't a curse, it was a privilege.

Greg had said that passion brought me there. Well, it wasn't my sodding passion, I can tell you that much. It had to be Eve's passion. I'd have to set things straight with her.

I don't remember how I got home. But at half past seven my alarm clock woke me up, and I was back in my own bed, and I felt exhausted, and my legs were aching from standing still too long.

During the lunch hour I set off to find Greg. As I approached his desk I could see he didn't recognise me at all, and that made my asking about our night time dalliances with his ex-girlfriend rather awkward. The look of angry bewilderment on his face spoke volumes, and I soon stammered to a halt; "See you tonight, then," I mumbled, and left. But I knew he'd been there in the bedroom with me, I hadn't imagined it. His eyes showed the same bloodshot sleeplessness mine had.

And I tracked down Eve. When she saw me, she sighed, and said, "I don't want to discuss this, I don't want to go out with you any more." It was odd to see that jaw move at last, and for all those words to spill out.

"Do you love me?" I said. "Because if you do, I think you should stop."

"I don't love you," she confirmed. "I have no feelings about you at all."

"Good," I said. "That's good. And you should know this then. I don't love you either."

She nodded at that. "Well, then," she said.

"Well," I agreed. And I actually thought that might have done the trick. I went to bed that night apprehensive but hopeful. But at two o'clock, it made no difference, the catapulting happened, I was back in position by her bedside. "Shit," I whispered, softly.

The next night I decided I simply wouldn't go to sleep. I drank lots of black coffee, litres of the stuff. And, yes, that kept me nicely alert for the catapulting moment – but it also meant that when I suddenly found myself standing over Eve Gershwin, I had the most agonising urge to piss. At the back of her bedroom, after my shift was done, I jogged up and down in my ghost costume, praying that dawn would soon come – and when my alarm clock rang and woke me from my own bedroom I nearly didn't make it to the toilet in time.

I didn't touch Eve at all for the first week. I want to make that clear. And when I finally decided to give it a go, really, it wasn't out of anything more passionate than boredom.

With my middle finger I carefully pressed down on her forehead. I thought it'd feel weird and syrupy, like the doorknob had, and it's true, it wasn't quite right, not quite like a forehead should feel – it yielded a bit too easily to my touch, wasn't there supposed to be bone underneath? But it was pleasant and warm.

I felt a bit ashamed, you know? And when I turned to look at my fellow ghosts I thought they might be judging me. But they weren't. Some nodded, some smiled. No one went as far as giving me a thumbs-up, or starting a round of applause – that would have broken that solemn church atmosphere they were so fond of – but they definitely approved. We knew the score, didn't we? All rejects of Eve Gershwin. Who wants to be in love, and get nothing back in return? Not that I was in love. I wasn't. But they were, the poor bastards. We were united by a common cause. Fuck it, we were *mates.*

And so, from that point on. If I thought I'd earned it, if I'd done a good day's work and deserved a treat. I don't know, if I just fucking felt like it. Some nights I might prod at Eve Gershwin's forehead for a bit.

It became harder to concentrate at the office. I'd start the morning with a renewed determination to do my best, to stay as bright and breezy as my new job demanded. By noon my eyelids were sinking and my head spun and my spirits felt as flat as a pancake.

Rather than take black coffee when I went to bed, I began popping sleeping pills. They wouldn't stop me materialising at Eve's house, but they took the edge off the boredom a bit, and the numbness that spread up my rigid standing body was comforting.

Eve wasn't always asleep. Those were the exciting nights. This one time she had insomnia, and was up for hours reading a book. If I leaned to the side, and strained my neck as far as it could go, I could read it alongside her. It was some sort of chick lit thing. It was shit, frankly, but beggars can't be choosers, and the storyline actually wasn't all that bad – but Eve was a faster reader than I was, and I'd rarely reached the end of a page before she'd turned over. It was hard to work out what was going on.

And once in a while she had sex. Those nights were exciting too, but I really wasn't sure where I was supposed to look. I discovered many things about Eve Gershwin it might have taken years of a real relationship to reveal – because I could see what her boyfriends couldn't, I could see the facial expressions when they'd turned away, or had their eyes closed, or were intent on nibbling at her nether regions. I learned that she liked her nipples tickled, she liked kissing at her thighs. Toe sucking, though, did nothing for her at all. And she wouldn't do anal for anyone.

There was this one guy she was sleeping with, a young lad, he didn't work at the office, I had no idea where Eve had found him. He kept on going for the toes. I wanted to say to him, you're barking up the wrong tree there, mate. All us ghosts knew his days were numbered. He didn't last long. One night he was chewing away at her feet, with Eve huffing away in irritation – the next, he was standing over her in a white sheet, as perplexed as hell, and crying with shock and disappointment.

I must admit, I liked it when we got new recruits. They were always so surprised to find themselves there, it made me laugh. I could see in contrast how well I had handled my own job deployment. I had been really good about it.

My Mum's birthday rolled around, then my Dad's.

My mum's birthday, then my Dad's. I didn't go to visit them. They were most put out. "But we don't know how many we'll have left!" I told them I was just too busy, sorry. And I really was, I had never been busier in my whole life! Besides Eve's birthday was looming, and we wanted to make it so special. The ghosts wouldn't be able to bring her presents or anything, we couldn't take objects with us, that wasn't how the catapulting worked. But we knew that night we'd stand watch over her that bit more protectively. That was the plan. But as it turned out – she didn't even show up. She didn't come home all night, her bed wasn't slept in. We all agreed she was probably out celebrating with a birthday shag – that gap year student in the mail room, we knew he'd been giving her the eye – and who could deny her that? Who could blame her? It was her birthday, after all. So we all sang happy birthday to her anyway. and pretended somehow she was able to hear. Greg gave a speech. He toasted Eve. And then he toasted us, that took me by surprise. He raised an imaginary glass to us all – we all followed suit. "To us, and another year of it! The best crew I've ever worked with! We're all in this together!" Some of us shed a tear. It was quite moving.

The very next day, I was called in to see the management. I was told that my work had been unsatisfactory for a while, and that if I couldn't handle the extra responsibility they could take away my promotion in an instant. I apologised, told them I would pull my socks up and work all the waking hours I had. And it was old Mr Ellis I had to promise this to, the fucking hypocrite.

That night as I stood over Eve Gershwin I pressed my finger on her forehead, I stabbed it down as hard as I could.

❖

At the end of summer, something broke.

I had gone to bed, washed and shaved, ready for my date with Eve, and my bladder was good and empty. And I don't know what happened, but when I stirred awake in the night I was still in my own house. It was already ten past two, and I was late. "Shit!" I said, and leaped out of bed. Thank God, I had at least transformed into a ghost, the white sheet was all around me, but it didn't alter the fact that my shift had already started the other side of town.

I phoned for a taxi. I was told there wouldn't be one for half an hour. "This is an emergency!" I yelled. "I'll pay double!" And a taxi was outside my house in five minutes flat. I'd put on a big anorak, the best to hide my ghost outfit, but the sheets were so big and billowy they kept popping out around my midriff.

I couldn't remember Eve's exact address. I'd spent every night there for the last six months, but I'd seen the outside of her house just the once. I asked the driver to go up and down likely looking roads; he kept trying to make conversation, and I had to tell him eventually to shut up. At that he dropped me off, and maybe that was just as well, I might find the place better on foot. I paid him his double fare, and a tip on top, and that didn't seem to mollify him at all.

All the houses were dark, and on those suburban streets they all looked the same. I admit it, I started to panic. I thought I'd have to give up and go home – and then I knew I *couldn't* give up, that was unacceptable. If necessary I would have to knock on people's doors, late as it was, and ask whether anyone might know where Eve Gershwin lived. And then – I turned a corner – and there it was. I couldn't be sure, but it was beside a lamp post, and the back garden I'd looked out on from Eve's window seemed familiar, and, yes, there was the graffiti on the pavement, the bins, the abandoned pram that never got moved.

And now what? I couldn't exactly ring the doorbell. I picked up some loose gravel, and threw them up at the upstairs window. And for a dread moment I thought I'd probably got the wrong house after all, and I prepared to run – but then, thank Christ, the faces of half a dozen ghosts came into view behind the pane, all shining white and ethereal, and peered down at me. I gave them a wave.

They couldn't open the front door, of course. No one could leave the bedroom. But the window was forced open. I took off my anorak, it would only weigh me down. And as my white sheets blew all around me in the night breeze, I shinned up the drainpipe.

"Where the hell have you been?" whispered Greg. "You've missed your turn. We had to give it to Terry." Terry was the ghost with the breast cupping fetish, and Terry grinned at me, I knew he wouldn't have minded the overtime.

The next night things were back to normal, and I was catapulted into Eve Gershwin's bedroom at two o'clock precisely the way I should have been. The night after, though, back on the blink. I phoned for a taxi. The taxi service remembered me, and said no. I phoned for a different taxi. It wasn't so bad, this time I knew how to get there. But I still missed the beginning of my shift, and still I had to climb up that fucking drainpipe.

The ghosts all seemed very disappointed in me, even the newbies. But I couldn't see how any of this was my fault.

The next day at work I received an envelope in the internal mail. Inside it was a house key. There was no note. I still don't know who sent it.

The other ghosts took the piss out of me, but I think they rather liked the fact I was properly solid and corporeal now. If nothing else, it meant I was the one who wasn't obliged to spend all night in the bedroom, and could nip to the kitchen and make cups of tea. "Anyone fancy a cuppa?" I'd say every half hour or so, and the ghosts would say yes, please, and I'd pop downstairs and brew us up a pot. I brought my own teabags, it didn't seem fair to use Eve's. And besides, she was into some weird herbal stuff, and we needed good old-fashioned bloke's tea if we were going to get through the long night.

Pretty soon things got worse. Not only did I wake me up in my own bedroom, I did so without a ghost costume. So I had to make my own. I got an old sheet, I cut out a hole for my head. I didn't do it in quite the right place, it was lopsided, and I kept tripping up over the train of it. But it was better than nothing, and even though the sheet was pretty grubby, after a few goes in the washing machine it gleamed nearly as white as my original.

And I didn't mind that I now looked different to the

other ghosts. Because I felt I'd been given a sort of promotion. It was my responsibility to keep them happy, I started to bring not just tea to work but chocolate digestives. And as dawn approached and the last ghost faded into thin air, downstairs I would take all the empty cups and plates and wash them up in the sink, keeping everything nice and tidy for when Eve got up. Then I'd let myself out and take care locking the front door behind me, I didn't want some weirdo getting in. Once in a while I'd leave her some breakfast. Bacon, eggs, toast, nothing too fancy, but you know, nice. I have no idea whether she enjoyed it or not.

The taxi fares cost a fortune, though, and I decided I'd have to rent somewhere closer to where Eve lived. That was a bitter shame. I'd loved my old house. If only I'd loved Eve Gershwin, it might have felt like a fair trade.

Then one day Eve Gershwin got herself a boyfriend again. I suppose I should have recognised the signs.

For a start, she hadn't been appearing in her bedroom all that much. The ghosts just had to sit around it drinking tea and eating biscuits without anything much to do. Greg said that Eve was probably visiting her parents, but that didn't seem likely, how often can anyone visit their parents? And she'd be in the office the next morning as usual. Still, Greg always seemed to know best.

It turned out that Eve was in love with Greg. They'd got back together somehow. Greg was all smiles around the office again, all laughter and bloke jokes, it was a bit nauseating to watch, if I'm honest. It appeared that Greg had been pulling a fast one on all of us. That whilst his ghost self spent the night with us guarding an empty bedroom, his actual body was out with Eve doing the nasty.

Eve looked happy too, I suppose. She was all smiles too. But I didn't trust those smiles. They didn't look as relaxed or as natural as the ones I'd seen on her sleeping face these past few months. I was an expert on her smiles. Greg had not been the man inside her head every night. I was sure of it. Greg was not the man of her dreams.

This is how we found out what was going on.

We were over at Eve's, the ghosts and I, and we'd settled ourselves in for a nice quiet evening. Not all of the lads had even shown up, there was no Mark, no Stuart or Alan, and Terry hadn't bothered for weeks now the breasts were in short supply. No Greg either, of course, and I found out the reason for that only too soon. And it was gone midnight, and we heard a key turn in the front door downstairs. "Action stations!" said old Mr Ellis, and the thinning collection of ghosts got into position ready to haunt.

In all the hurry I'd forgotten to clean up the cups of tea, but Eve didn't seem to mind. Her attentions were elsewhere. She entered the bedroom already wrapped around Greg's body, and they were kissing each other with such hunger, now tearing off each other's clothes then throwing them on to the floor. The ghosts watched on aghast, and who could blame us? We'd never seen our Eve show such frenzy before. She certainly never had with any of us – and then they were naked, and they were at it full pelt, and Eve was crying out, and she *never* cried out, she had been a discreet and disinterested lover – and Greg was all over her nipples and all over her ears, and was giving the toes a wide berth. And I thought as I watched him, he's *studied* for this, this is what these past few months have been for – he wasn't protecting Eve at all, he was getting insider information!

And then, slowly, distinctly, as they both reached climax, Greg raised one hand high in the air. Pointed directly at where he knew the ghosts stood to watch. And gave us all the finger.

Was I jealous of Greg? Well, let's get this clear. Absolutely not. One hundred per cent not, no, no way. Greg may have been an utter knob, but fair play to him, he'd been clever, he'd turned the situation to his advantage. But for me? Let me put it like this. The more time I spent with Eve. Watching over her as she slept. Seeing what she's like when she thought she was alone. The better I got to know her – it's weird, it's *funny* – I knew her less and less. How can that make sense? And isn't that the exact opposite of love, really? Every night Eve ate away at me bit by bit – all the parts of me that might have loved her, that might have cared for her even just a scrap. And I hated her stupid girly voice, and I hated the toothy way she smiled, and I hated the little gasp she made every single time she came, seriously, it sounded so artificial, I'm so relieved we never actually had sex, I'd have punched her. No, hate is too strong a word, I didn't *hate* her – I'll put it this way, I had no strong feelings about Eve whatsoever. Really. Not at all. So, you know, good luck to Greg, he was welcome to her. I didn't love Eve, and I'd never loved Eve – but if I *had* ever loved Eve, let's just say if I had, then that was over for good. Beautiful as she was, and Eve was beautiful, alarmingly beautiful, she was in all ways alarming – with all that beauty, lying there in bed every night, and me standing watch and pressing my finger down upon her warm syrupy forehead – she may have been gorgeous to everybody else, but to me Eve Gershwin was nothing more now than a slab of fucking meat.

So I said, "I think our work here is done, lads," and the ghosts agreed that any practical use our hauntings may have had, they'd reached their natural conclusion. We tried to work out some way to mark the occasion. "I could cut her hair off," I said. "Shall I cut her hair off? I want to cut her hair off." Some of the ghosts looked unhappy at my suggestion, so I went on to explain. "I didn't mean *all* her hair. Just the odd strand, and we can keep them, like mementoes. Like trophies, even. No, not trophies, that sounds fucking creepy, mementoes, like mementoes." I went to fetch some scissors from the kitchen, but then I saw this steak knife, and I thought, fuck yes. Eve and Greg were fast asleep, snuggled tightly together so close they were both on the same pillow. It was almost cute, and I had to take care I was cutting the right head! I began to slice away, and all the ghosts put in requests, and then I passed around these thick clumps of Eve's hair, and we knew it was the end of an era, and everyone looked sad, and everyone looked happy too. We wished each other all the best, as if we were never going to see each other again, as if half of us wouldn't be in the office together the next morning – but that didn't matter, this was *ours right now*, never to be discussed or acknowledged again, this special moment was *ours*, and we deserved it, we'd taken good care of Eve Gershwin, she had nothing to complain about. And we weren't too embarrassed to put our clumps of hair up to our noses and give them a big fat sniff – really fill up our nasal passages with as much of Eve as we could get, it made our heads spin, it was great. And then we shook hands goodbye , and some of us hugged. Our vigil was done.

Or rather, their vigil was done. I had no intention of giving up on it. I just didn't want the other ghosts getting in my way.

I kept the largest clump of hair for myself. I kept the steak knife too.

Mr Ellis interrupted work to make a special announcement. He said he was delighted to inform us that there was going to be a marriage in the company! And that at five o'clock there'd be champagne so we could all toast the engagement of Greg Murphy and Eve Gershwin. Ellis actually looked pleased. I don't know how he managed it. Ellis, who had been so distraught. Ellis, whose ghost had sat down on the floor beside the bed and cried.

The champagne was in paper cups. We all toasted the couple, and said we hoped they'd be very happy together. But Eve Gershwin does not make men happy. She is not a woman to inspire joy.

I hadn't spoken to Eve in a long while. I saw her each night for work, it would have been exhausting having to see her in the daylight as well. But as everybody else was going up to her to wish her congratulations, I thought I should take the opportunity to have a word.

She looked up at me expectantly over the paper cup. She even smiled a bit. Everything forgiven now, and all ready to accept my well wishes.

"You loved me once," I said. "I know you fucking did, that's why you made me haunt you. And I get that it's over for you, but you don't get to say when it's over for me. And I won't give up. I shall still watch over you. I shall still protect you. Every single night. Do you think all I'm going to get is a kiss? When I see what else you've been getting up to, you slut. You whore, you slut." But I said it all really gently, you know, so she'd know I cared. Like it was a promise.

She went white at that, and it was as if I was seeing what *her* ghost looked like. Still beautiful – even with those bald patches in her hair, it made her look like she'd got alopecia.

Greg came up to me in the toilets as I was washing my hands. And I decided to forgive Greg. I had been used, all the ghosts had been used – but, fair enough, you know me well enough to know I'm not the sort of bloke who holds a grudge. "Hello, Greg," I said, amiably enough, "the two of you fucking deserve each other." He grabbed me and held my face hard against the mirror, my nose squashed on the glass, it chipped a tooth. It hurt. "You just leave her alone," he said. "Do you hear me? You leave her the fuck alone!" And he made it pretty clear he wouldn't release me until I promised I would.

But I didn't know it was a promise I could keep. Some force compelled me each night to visit Eve Gershwin as she slept. I didn't know what that force was, precisely. All I knew, it was no longer a supernatural one.

I tried very hard.

I want you to understand that. I always tried so very, very hard.

But pretty soon my body was itching for my ghost costume. Yearning for it even, I didn't feel complete until it was around me. I didn't feel like I was properly myself. Peeping out of the two little eye holes I had cut into the sheets, and seeing the world behind that thin little carapace of white, I felt I could get a grasp on it. I felt protected.

I almost didn't need to do anything else. Could just have shut myself off away from it all, hidden beneath the sheet, I wouldn't have had to do anything, I wouldn't have had to accept the slightest bit of responsibility, not towards Eve, not towards myself, even. I could have just stayed in my own bed, for the first time in so very long, and waited for dawn.

Oh, my God. Even now, that sounds so sweet. So delicious. Oh. Believe me.

I have a regular taxi driver. I like him. He's never tried to make conversation. He never shows any emotion at all. Tonight, though, I surprise him when I tell him where I want to go.

And there I am, standing outside Alice's house. Her bedroom light is still on. Oh yes, that's right, I remember, she was always a late night owl. I have to wait until the house is dark, then wait another good half hour so everything will be nice and still.

It's cold. I miss the summer. Things were better then. But my summer with Eve is gone, and you have to move on, don't you? What's the alternative? That way madness lies. So very cold, I hug myself beneath my white sheet.

I wonder how Alice is. I haven't seen her in ages.

I wonder if she's warm.

I still have a spare key. It doesn't work. She has changed the locks! Well, what do you make of that! So I have to do what I have never done to Eve's house. I smash a window to get inside.

I remember Alice's bedroom, going in there gives me a rush of nostalgia. There isn't the scented soap and perfume of Eve's room, but there's still something female about it, something sweet to smell. We once had sex in this room quite a lot. She hasn't done anything about the headboard, I notice. When we'd had sex, the headboard would thump.

Alice is snoring. It's definitely snoring. Her face doesn't smile as it snores. Instead, it contorts into a sort of frown, a confused frown, as if she's concentrating on her dream very hard indeed but isn't at all convinced by what she finds in there. But she isn't thrashing the way she could sometimes do. She is calm. Calm, at least, for Alice.

Those buck teeth of hers. She really is fucking plain. But then, so am I. We are complementarily fucking plain.

I check my watch. It is ten past two. All right, then, we'll say this is a two o'clock shift, and from now on I'll make sure to arrive on time and get into position ten minutes earlier. It won't matter this once. And besides, I can put in a bit of overtime to make up for it.

The blade of the steak knife against my finger. It doesn't feel sharp. It feels syrupy.

I set the knife down on the bedside table. I don't need it. I won't let myself need it. Not tonight, anyway.

No, I shall protect Alice. From anything that might cause her harm. From all the monsters and ghouls and ghosts in the world.

And I reach out a finger, my middle finger. And press it down, hard, firm, right upon her forehead.

Midsummer Eve

Jenn Ashworth

'Nothing yet from the embassy, John?' Terry asked. He was the type of man that called any male who served him 'John', and was so absorbed in his own business that he hadn't noticed the reception desk was empty until he'd already spoken. He leaned against the polished counter.

'John?'

Funny that. John was there just a second ago, his neat clean smile signalling he was ready to assist. But Terry could have been thinking of this morning, actually, and another John entirely. If Terry was going to tell the truth, he had to admit he couldn't confidently tell the Johns apart. Not in a racist way: they all, despite the heat, wore the same white shirts and silk waistcoats. It was the uniform that made each John hard to tell from the next – not their skin colour. And relying on context didn't help – he could no longer think of this one as *the reception John* and that one as *the bar John* and the other as *the turndown service John* because the diminished team were all doing double duty now, *the shoe shine John* turning up with the morning newspaper, and *the mango sorbet by the pool John* sometimes appearing in the suite to get his evening bath started.

'Nobody there?'

Alone in the massive, sparkling lobby, he shook his head with careful regret. This was no way to treat a client. He'd see about this. Make a complaint. Client was the wrong word. He was a guest: he and Tilly both. They were guests of this hotel. The best hotel on the island, it was, standing alone on the southern edge, overlooking the lagoon. You could even say, given the hotel's position on the island and the island's position relative to the mainland (beyond the lagoon, on the island's southern aspect there lay nothing but thousands of miles of clear blue ocean) this was the best hotel in a three thousand mile radius. Give or take. Terry should give them that one for the brochure. He looked over his shoulder. No Johns to be seen anywhere.

'Hello? Service?'

He should not, given what he had paid and was probably still paying, through no fault of his own, be treated as just any guest. One in a line of guests. He expected, despite everything, standards to be maintained. The highest standards of hospitality. The island in general, its people, and this hotel in particular, was famous for it. Hadn't they advertised that very thing in the brochure? Impeccable service? Every need anticipated and fulfilled? Well what Terry needed now was the embassy or the travel insurance company or any one of a number of people Tilly had been phoning in the last few weeks to step in and handle this situation.

'John?'

A fly buzzed around his ear and he waved it away. It was no good, that. No good at all. The lobby was silent –

other than the regular swish-sweep of the overhead fan and the bubble of the somewhat murky aquarium. Standards were dropping, just slightly – you saw it in these tiny details – others wouldn't notice but a man like Terry – a man used to the finer things and who had learned to expect them (given the price he had paid and was almost certainly still paying) noticed that the inside of the aquarium was growing a skin of algae and the fish inside, bubble mouthed and candy-coloured, were starting to look unhappy. Nobody in this hotel should have anything other than a blissed-out smile on their faces at all times, not at these prices.

'I'm going to the pool,' he called, on the off-chance John was lying stretched out behind the counter recovering from a fainting fit and on the brink of returning to his post. 'If the embassy send a message...'

There was no answer. Terry waved his hand around his head. These insects. Inside the hotel. His skin burned and, despite the smooth expensive swish of the fan overhead (which was just for the show of it – this was the type of hotel that had hot and cold air laid on invisibly in every room and you could – if you could work it out – control it from your smart phone) it was too hot. He'd never meant to be here until full summer.

'Never mind, John,' he called cheerfully, guessing that he was probably on a security camera somewhere, and not wanting to look a fool. 'I'll just go for a swim. Tell my wife where I am if you see her, will you?'

Terry turned and walked through the wide spotless glass doors. It could only be a matter of days now. Hadn't the hotel manager himself, on a rare personal visit to the establishment and during an unprecedented gathering of the guests – a small crowd, they were, back then, in the main entertainment suite – bowed deeply, many times, and promised that they would be – each of them, all of them – taken great care of. Hadn't he said – hadn't he *promised* – that the embassies of their respective nations would almost certainly sort something out? The international picture was unresolved and fast moving, he said, in perfect English, then again in perfect French, Italian, Swiss. But most governments of rich countries were chartering planes, sending vouchers, making some sort of arrangement – it would just take time, that's all. And in the meantime, they all remained – would remain – honoured guests. Over the following days – Terry had lost count of how many – the hotel had slowly emptied, the staff thinned out, and standards – Terry regretted to note – had steadily declined.

He hesitated. Should he perhaps pop upstairs and get Tilly himself? She'd be having a lie-down, or putting something on her face, or getting a hair treatment. Was almost certainly lying in bed with her face in a book, or hunched in front of her tablet trying to read the news, or soaking her feet in bowls of iced rosewater and complaining – *complaining* – about the heat. She should, Terry had advised, make the most of this. Extended honeymoon. Holiday of a lifetime and, more than likely, the tab picked up by Her Majesty's government.

She couldn't say they hadn't been looked after. Every night, every single night without fail, the two of them were served their full five courses out on the terrace, their lonely table crowned with flowers, candles, the works. Four serving waiter Johns all to themselves, and a violinist John between courses, making music a respectful distance away. A rose for the lady. Every night. What had she to complain about? They couldn't provide every single choice on the menu, not on a reduced staff, but still, it was pretty good. Apart from the insects that is, which of course outdoors and in the evening were to be expected – one of the natural hazards of the tropical environment, he supposed, though the agent had not mentioned them and neither had the brochure, and he had already made a note of that. No, Terry thought, decisively leaving the hotel and walking briskly along crazy paved paths so carefully swept there was no real need for shoes – he'd go to the pool on his own and leave Tilly upstairs.

Terry reached his preferred lounger. It was set up as he liked it, the rolled towel at the end for his feet, the table set out ready with his paper, his water, his iced fruit platter. They had a knack, these Johns, for coming and going invisibly. It was high quality, that.

The pool was kidney bean shaped, the water cool and still and bright. He admired the colour of it, the bright flowers in the shrubbery, the discreet towel bins. It was the sort of life a man could get used to. Though it had been a while now. Three months of the lounger, and cocktails on the terrace, and paperbacks on the beach, and five-star meals on silver service, and a steady stream of news from home and the rest of the world coming through on Tilly's phone. And now it was

Midsummer's Eve and the heat was becoming difficult, the insects unbearable, and Tilly was in all probability still sulking in the room because she was too hot and she wanted to go home. He arranged himself on his preferred lounger then called into the empty air.

'Will you take a message up to my Tilly? Tell her I'll wait down here for her?'

He didn't wait for an answer.

'She's up in the room. Headache. Leg ache. Face ache!'

He laughed. You could say what you liked to these people. English perfect – every single one of them. It was part of the training, he supposed. More languages between them than Soft Mick but they had discretion too, and knew when to turn a blind ear. The service was unobtrusive to a fault. He was, as he unbuttoned his shirt and kicked off his beach shoes, about to launch into what Tilly would have called 'one of his diatribes' (he wasn't totally confident she knew what the word meant, or where she'd have picked it up) about her wandering off out of the resort, off in search of shops, or souvenirs, and yes, he knew a place like this – catering to the clientele it did – was probably safer than the high-street back home at pub kicking out time (and he wouldn't let her wander alone and unsupervised at night in Didcot either, not a woman like her – with her looks, he meant) but with the taxi drivers gone, downed tools, and all the shops shut, the resort generally and the hotel particularly was really the best place for her. He was about to say all this. Then, suddenly tired, he lay on his preferred lounger and closed his eyes.

The sun tightened the skin on his face. Three whole months of heaven on earth with the angelic Johns and the pool was about as far as he got, these days. At the start of their honeymoon, he'd taken Tilly to the beach every day. That was the main attraction of a place like this: the white, unspoiled sand. That's what had been advertised in the brochure and that's what they'd got. They made full use of it, despite the crowds.

Some days, early on, you could hardly see the sand between the spread-out beach towels and white, slowly burning flesh. Topless women too, though Terry hadn't expected it to be that sort of place, nobody was going to catch him complaining. He just didn't let Tilly catch him looking. This was their honeymoon after all. As the situation with travel and curfews and quarantines progressed the resort gradually emptied and he'd insisted on taking advantage of it by going to the beach more often, and staring for longer. Tilly had got as brown as he'd ever seen her and Terry himself enjoyed it more now that there was no competition for the sun loungers, no sellers and hawkers disturbing their peace.

He stood on the hot sand sometimes looking past the bent palm trees and the surf and the sea – light blue darkening to navy – little fishes twitching in the shallows like a real life nature documentary – something by Attenborough – and felt like he owned the place. In the absence of any other non-John humans to lay a claim (the resort really did empty out that fast – down to the fuss the press made, no doubt) in some sense, now he did.

But eventually, with just the two of them, and the

weeks progressing into full summer, it was too strange and too hot and they stayed by the pool and worked through the pile of tattered paperbacks left in the bar by the tourists who'd managed to get themselves home. John would come out every hour or so to offer them drinks and nibbles, and Terry, after checking whether they were on the house, part of the all-inclusive deal, or to be paid for (he was no fool) accepted them. They slept a lot while the rest of the world – a world that existed very far away – fell into chaos. Tilly cried a lot and spent a lot of time on her phone. The sun gave them both migraines and sometimes they lost whole days to their headaches.

Terry sat up. The little fruit platter by his elbow had been replenished. He helped himself, feeling a cold wet slice of some strange tropical thing on his tongue. He should go easy on Tilly. None of this was her fault. Maybe she wasn't sulking, but sleeping off her poorly head. He still felt a bit dodgy himself. He'd spent most of the previous day – or was it days? – in the hotel room, turning and turning in damp cotton sheets and having bad daytime sleeps where he woke sweating, into a nightmare, then woke again, sweating, from that nightmare – the dreams boxed up one inside the other like those tricky foreign dolls you could buy in toyshops. The beach wasn't far away: maybe tomorrow. Today the pool was enough.

Because even though (he put an arm over his eyes) he probably should be in bed himself, he wasn't going to waste the day. He'd told Tilly to make the best of it and had done his best to show her a good time and a positive example. It was no wonder they had argued: her attitude left a lot to be desired. Tilly had spent a lot of what was prime man and wife alone time, in one of the most exclusive resorts in the world, now enjoyed entirely by them only (the thought that they were the most waited-on honeymooning couple in the entire world occurred to him regularly, and the thrill did not dissipate by dint of repetition) glued to her phone, eating up news of home. She watched video clips of the roadblocks and the riots. The police patrolling the public places. The pictures of ambulances queuing outside hospitals, and doctors and nurses sleeping sitting up in hospital corridors or sprawled out like dead bodies on spattered operating theatre floors.

'Just tell me if the embassy emails and keep the rest of that nonsense to yourself,' he'd said, lain back on his lounger and twitched his hat over his face. But Tilly inhaled the articles and insisted on giving him little tit-bits from the headlines. Daily counts of the infected, the sick, the hospitalised, the dead. There were graphs, though he didn't hold with that sort of thing. Anybody with a computer could make numbers mean anything they liked, after all.

'They've run out of body bags,' she said. And once, 'they're digging mass graves. Outside Luton.'

'Terrible airport, Luton,' Terry had replied. 'Make sure they don't fly us back there. I want Heathrow or nothing. When they get in touch.'

He will admit now, in retrospect, he was trying to annoy her.

'Do you think they'll fly us back first class?' he asked. 'We paid for first class.' Tilly didn't answer.

The army sprayed the ports and airports with disinfectant, then they closed them. They'd missed their original flight home, of course. Or it had been cancelled. It was hard to keep hold of the details. The Johns brought parasols and chilled towels and little cucumber water sprays and apologised, bowing deeply, for current events and the climate, but none of those things were any help at all.

It wasn't that Terry lacked sympathy. Terrible shame for those who were sick, both here and at home. Unprecedented, obviously, though no need for the press – he'd seen the headlines of the English language newspapers while they were still being delivered and fanned out on one of the shiny tables in the breakfast room – and the fuss they were all making. The drama. Fomenting was a word he'd been keeping in store for a time like this.

'Don't bring me the papers anymore, John,' he'd decided one morning, over his full English (they provided a good enough version of the traditional classic). 'They're fomenting unrest!' He jerked his head at Tilly, who was weeping over her fruit salad. The Johns had made a special effort over that fruit salad – everything she brought to her mouth was in the shape of a flower. She left most of it untouched, and it was down to the newspapers, so Terry made his executive decision and they stopped appearing.

There was just no need for it. The things they'd been

printing. Hadn't they all had coughs? Some of the Johns. Housemaids, sneezing and red-faced in the hallways. On the last night they'd had proper entertainments one of the dancers had keeled right over, her feathery headdress coming undone and falling off the front of the stage. The compere John could not apologise enough. But if you got some rest and fluids inside you and didn't play silly beggars, no worse than a bad cold, after all. He'd suffered himself and not made such a song and dance about it.

He and Tilly had both had sore throats, tight chests, and on the second or third day, a fever that had brought both of them to their beds. Mango sorbet by the pool John had intuitively, silently diversified and brought hot black tea and fresh towels and jugs of ice. By this time the hotel had closed its doors and the housemaids had been at a loose end so they'd also had their bed sheets changed and bathroom scrubbed twice daily. 'Treated like royalty,' he'd said to Tilly, who was burning up, her eyes dark and glassy.

One day – a week or two days or a month or six weeks back, it was impossible to tell the days apart from each other now – Terry had been swimming in the pool when one of the Johns had come and motioned him towards the edge. He'd made his way over, half wading, half breast-and-belly-stroking along, until the water slopped over the lip of the pool and lapped at John's feet. It wasn't like them to interrupt your relaxation in that way. The waiters had not relaxed their standards – not where it counted – and he was still wearing the shiny black lace-up shoes that came with the hotel uniform.

'A call, Sir,' John said. He was holding a tray – one of the little round black plastic trays from the bar. But instead of a brightly coloured cocktail with fruit in it (Tilly) or a bottle of beer, condensation beaded down the glass (him) there was a cordless phone and he tried to reach for it – tried to reach for the phone, with the impression that if he could just get that phone into his hand, and get one of the Johns to come – to get some help for he and Tilly both – well then things would be fine. But he was so hot, and so tired, and every muscle in his body ached (the sunburn, and the swimming – which he was unused to – he supposed) and the bed sheet caught around his elbow, and it felt easier just to lie back, and let the phone lie in its cradle, and after a while the urge had gone away and he had slept. The water sloshed against his ears and no matter how he arranged the pillows he couldn't get comfortable. Tilly was crying – he could hear her, but he had no time to deal with her today.

Terry got up from his preferred lounger, feeling the heat in his skin. He'd pay for that later. But right now, a dip in the water would be just the ticket. It was silent now: you'd imagine there'd be monkeys in the trees or fancy birds talking or squawking or flying about, but there was nothing like that. The water was cool and soothing and he lowered himself in gently. Sometimes, on days like this as he dozed in the hot sun or swam endless laps around the small pool, he wondered about the bill he was racking up. Was he eating every meal in the hotel bar now? Were they still setting up the table for them on the terrace? They should still be getting room service, shouldn't they?

Things between he and Tilly would be fine. Two people crammed in close to each other, in these circumstances, with no other company – well, they were bound to get on each other's nerves a bit. He'd tried to get her out – gave her the credit cards and told her to visit the salon or get someone to the room to do her hair and her feet – but she was still getting over her cough and wasn't in the mood, then when she seemed to be feeling a bit better she'd gone quiet on him – and whether this was the way she was when she was very relaxed, or the prelude to an argument, he could not tell. All the extra amenities in the resort – the ones he was paying an arm and a leg for – closed down. He managed to wangle them some complementary room service – some bottles of champagne and breakfasts on the hotel – in respect of the diminished services, less than the brochure had promised – but she was still upset. No evening entertainments. No masseuse. No cooking demonstrations or scuba driving trips. It wasn't what he'd promised her. He did know that. Still, she needed to show a bit of Blitz spirit. Show these people how the English did things. He swam another lap, the backs of his toes scraping the bottom of the pool uncomfortably as he reached the shallow end, paused, then turned. The water slopped at his ears and he lifted his chin proud of the water and continued.

He missed her. His Tilly. Strange to say that, given they were on their honeymoon. He was – it had come to him late in life, unexpectedly, and now he was like a big soft lad and he'd have to watch himself or she'd have the upper hand for the rest of their lives together – besotted with her. He thought about her all the time. He needed her. It had not been the best honeymoon. He'd admit that. They'd both taken to sleeping during the day – there was hardly anything else to do other than eat the things the invisible Johns brought on the trays, and lie by the pool – no newspapers now, and the internet not working properly, at first not enough, and then not at all – so of course they dozed, and yesterday or the day before – perhaps last week – woke unexpectedly in the hot sun and felt sick and dehydrated. They had to traipse, sunburn itching, through the hotel and up in the lift and back to their room. At the door Tilly had said, 'let's not go in there' and for the first time in what seemed like a long time, had touched his arm. He'd forgotten she was with him, in the lift, right beside him – but where else would she be but by his side, the two of them here together in this five star place, on their honeymoon, heaven on earth, starting off in luxury as man and wife – the luxury she should get used to, he liked to joke. He looked at her reflection in the mirror.

They were still in the lift, or they'd got out of it and were in the hotel lobby, with the big clean gold-edged mirrors everywhere (was it gilt? Was that the right word?) or they'd got out of the lift on the wrong floor, or they were still in bed, looking at themselves in the mirrored wardrobes – he can't remember now – but he looked at her in the mirror, wan and pale beside him, her eyes all black, and she touched his arm and her hand was cold and her touch made him shiver all over and he thought *get a handle on that, Terry, or she'll have you under her thumb forever.* He was going to shrug her off but because in his heart of hearts he didn't want to, he couldn't make himself, and anyway her hand felt deliciously cold against his skin and it made him remember his sunburn, and he made a note to himself to ask John to get him some more sun-cream. Some of that aloe vera stuff. The good stuff, the stuff the locals use. But that won't be right. They must make it for the tourists. The locals won't have sun cream will they, they'll be used to it. He hasn't seen any locals. Only the Johns, and a maid or two, and not even a maid for a couple of days. Maybe longer. His thinking wasn't working properly. He was dreaming, or inside a dream of a dream again, and Tilly was always there – at the edge of his vision, or walking away, or vanishing as the lift doors closed and swept him away from her – and he felt the water against his chest and arms and submerged himself, letting the water fill his ears, then pushed upwards, making splashing noises.

'Not there,' Tilly had said, he was sure of that, and she'd clutched at his arm and he let himself be guided back to the lift or was it to bed and yes, it hadn't been the honeymoon he'd promised her but it wasn't like they'd got the flu on purpose, was it? There was a buzzing noise, the insects terrible, and so early in the day, and he shook his head then ducked it under the water again. It was the only proper escape from them. He should ask John for a breathing tube. A little scuba mask and pipe. A decent John would have thought of that already. Standards had declined slightly: he wasn't going to pretend he hadn't noticed. But that special skill the waiters and maids and so on had – of being both at your elbow and anticipating your every need and entirely invisible – like fairies, Tilly said, delighted by the rose petals that appeared on the bed while she was bathing on the second night – was nearly magical. And they were (he recalled the tray on the edge of the pool, the jug of iced water, the little silver dish of mango sorbet they'd worked out – as if by occult means – was his favourite) doing their best to keep it up: the illusion it was business as usual. The water closed in around him, cool, but not unpleasantly so. They got that right, this hotel – the water temperature. He couldn't fault it. Cooled you without chilling you. Neither of them were that good with the heat. That's why they'd booked early – middle of March, which would be a nice spring. Plenty hot enough for English people, the agent had said. And then the flu, and now it was coming into full summer. Midsummer's Eve, was it? It must have been months.

He should go and find her. He waded across to the ladder and emerged, water streaming from his mouth and nostrils, running down his legs and evaporating the moment it hit the tiles, so he didn't even leave a footprint.

'Tilly?'

He saw his Tilly sometimes, as he emerged from the water, his eyes cloudy with chlorine. She was sitting at a table with her sunhat and glasses on, a paperback novel in her hand. Or she was leaning against the closed bar, sipping at a cocktail, a flower in her hair. Once – thrillingly – he saw her in one of the poolside showers, as naked as a baby, the water running down her back as she washed her hair. He was about to shout at her – tell her to get some clothes on – she was for his eyes only, after all, then laughed at himself. Who was there to see? Only the Johns, and they wouldn't dare – not at this sort of hotel. She was a walking fantasy, was his Tilly. His princess. How had he got hold of someone like her? For the life of him he could not remember. He called to her a few times but she kept her back to him, soaping her hair for a long time, and when he wiped his eyes, she was gone. Where was she now? There wasn't anywhere to go. The main restaurant had closed, and the tennis courts shut up and the instructor gone home, and all the evening entertainments cancelled and if he was paying this extra bill – which he wasn't, Her Majesty's Government could see to that – he'd expect the lack of evening entertainments to be reflected in the price.

The tray was there, next to his preferred lounger. A fresh fruit platter, and a phone. The Johns were always leaving phones out for him. He didn't like it. Didn't like the thought of the strange black object in his hand. He stared at it. It was a reminder of home, of the business, of all the work left undone. But that wasn't it. Something else? Something Tilly wanted him to do. Or wished he'd done. He reached for his shirt, ignoring the tray, and when he turned back to retrieve his beach shoes it was gone, the discreet John having received the message loud and clear. No phones.

Terry found himself still lying on his preferred lounger. He made himself get up – stand up properly before he fell asleep again – and saw it was evening. It got dark suddenly here; the lamps around the pool gently dimmed then switched off by unseen hands. Beyond the pool was the terrace, where he and Tilly had been taking their evening meals – simpler and simpler as the days passed, the romantic quartet dwindling to a single violinist, who himself faded into the surf and the dark until Terry could hardly remember him being there at all. And beyond the terrace's lamp-lit crazy paving, dark now, a low-whitewashed wall it would be easy to climb over, and beyond that, the beach, palm trees, the sea.

There was a faint pink glow at the horizon – like the dregs of a sunset, and not – and when that flickered out, the sea and the beach disappeared. Terry rubbed the back of his head with the towel, still staring out at what he could not see. He could sense it – the vastness of the expanse of water, black as treacle now, and softly lapping at the sand the brochure had promised would be white and unspoilt. He took a step or two towards the terrace, towards the wall, towards the sand and the sea, remembering the remoteness of this island, the way that on its southward aspect, there was nothing at all between the sea-view windows of the hotel and the southern edge of the entire world but water. A few weeks ago – give or take – he'd seen a cruise ship out there. It was after the trouble had started and the ports were turning the ships back, so they had nowhere to go.

'He's out of his way, John,' Terry had remarked. The

John had silently agreed. The boat – a big white liner – had gone back and forth a couple of times, making some kind of distress call with its horn and ruining the atmosphere – and then it had gone back to wherever it had come from. John hadn't thought about it since, not up until now. There were no horns sounding tonight. The black water out there was invisible to him, but he could hear it sloshing back and forth. He could go down there now, he supposed. A night swim. He couldn't remember if the brochure had said anything about sharks. Stinging floating things in the surf. But no. Tilly would be upstairs, waiting. Wanting him to get showered and get a jacket on so they were decent for their dinners. He would do what she wanted. It was her honeymoon and he wanted to make sure she had nothing to complain about. He turned away and walked around the pool, back towards the hotel.

He and Tilly had not seen eye-to-eye about everything on their honeymoon. He had perhaps, Terry reflected, been a little harsh at times. She couldn't be blamed, in the circumstances. As the time wore on, each day a few minutes longer than the last, and nothing to mark the changes except the rotation in meals (simpler as the days went on, but still served on the terrace, impeccable service from the waiter Johns, he must note that) tempers were bound to fray. She'd been on the phone to the embassy. To the travel insurance people. Both offices overwhelmed, of course. Engaged tone more often than not, and no messages returned as yet. There'd been calls to his son – at international rates, no less – back in Didcot, who was running the business. Things needed to be taken care of. Tilly did most of it – he wasn't really a phone person. But there were nice facilities for wives: the evening entertainments, a spa, two saunas and a beautician and hairdresser who'd come to the room. There was a shop. Perfumes and scarves and earrings and so on. Plenty for her to be getting on with. She, on balance, had no grounds for being disappointed.

Tonight he'd put on his jacket and tell her to get her nice dress on and get John to provide some music. Some proper English tunes. Things she'd recognise. The Johns would be able to do that. And it would cheer her up. They'd get what they were paying for. Still paying for, until the insurance or the embassy intervened. He'd have to ask for an itemised receipt. He made a note of it. As he reached the hotel he saw that the main lights in the reception were out, the wide atrium lit by some fluorescent strips above the doors. Emergency generator. It gave the place an unwelcoming appearance.

'Power cut, Tilly,' he said. 'Can't be helped. Tropical storm, or something along those lines.'

Still in his towel, which was slightly against the hotel's rules, he wandered through the reception area towards the lifts. Nobody called out. Nobody greeted him or humbly, tactfully reminded him about the buttoned shirt and shoes policy. Still, as the last remaining guests, they'd felt comfortable taking a certain amount of leeway, and expecting a certain latitude given.

'John? Where are you? John?'

His voice did not echo. He hardly heard it at all. Must be something to do with the carpet – which was as thick and spotless and soft as you'd expect for an establishment like this – and the walls, which were of some pale, veined marble-like material – probably a plastic veneer of some kind (he made a note of this – would check properly the next time he came through) and absorbed all sound. He made his way towards the lift, the doors of which stood open.

The thing is (even in the lift, the insects were intolerable, buzzing around his face with their high-pitched, machine-like whine) Tilly needed to be more understanding. They'd both taken this cough thing pretty hard, and it wasn't his fault that the airports and so on had closed. They'd made the best of it. He turned to explain this to her, before remembering she was in their room. He emerged from the lift, feeling or remembering feeling or dreaming her hand on his arm, pulling him back.

'Not here, Terry. Not in there.'

Her voice came gently but he could tell she was irritated. Had been irritated. She'd told him this before.

'Not here.'

He went on along the corridor regardless. One room was as good as another in a hotel like this. She'd been so excited about choosing when he'd shown her the brochure. The remoteness – the isolation and unspoilt nature of the island – had been its main selling point. Reflected in the price. She didn't care about the rooms at all. It was the island she wanted – the loneliness of it. He was flattered by it – she wanted to be alone with him.

Have him entirely to herself. It was not often you found yourself wanted like that and he'd given her what she wanted. This place, and himself. She wanted him to herself, and she could have him. An insect flew past his ear. Landed on his arm. They never bit you. He'd noticed that, of late. They started off biting you, and you needed the cream and the repellent and what have you, but after a while they got used to you or you got used to them, and they stopped biting. The midges or mosquitoes, or whatever the local word for them was, tended to leave them alone now. They'd fly around, gather in clouds, and he could hear them – hear them more or less all the time, these days ('Can you hear that, Tilly? Driving me mental,' he'd said in bed one night, and she'd hardly raised her head from the pillow, she was so hot and tired, but only blinked at him and smiled, her eyes sticky.) The fly – it was a fly – just an old-fashioned blue bottle, the same as they had at home – they were unclean, those sorts of flies. They landed on shit and rubbed their legs about in it and picked it up on their feet and then landed on your food or cutlery and the hotel was very good about hygiene, all the dishes on the breakfast buffet covered in silver cloches the morning John would lift up to display the food, when you asked him – even when he and Tilly were the only ones going down; that was a nice touch, that, and he'd note it – anyway, the point was, mosquitoes were a natural feature of the tropical environment and as such, couldn't be reflected in the tip, or otherwise noted, but bluebottles – blue-arsed flies, as his dad called them, like the ones at home on Didcot tip – and in such a quantity as this, well, that was certainly unacceptable and he would make a note of it. One of the buggers landed on his arm. He swept it away with a hand as he padded along the endless corridor. Or was that her hand now, cool on his sunburn?

'Tilly? You there?'

She wasn't talking to him. Hadn't been, really, for a while now. She should have nothing to complain about. This wasn't the sort of place where girls like her ended up – not outside of fairy tales and the more sentimental kind of film. Every morning, the clean towels folded up into bears or pigs or swans or what have you, and roses in the bedroom, endless minibar (included) and a cigar on a napkin on the table on the balcony, just for him. The brochure didn't call the place heaven on earth for nothing – and no, they hadn't expected to be here so long, not until full summer, but he couldn't be blamed for that. They weren't the only couple to have faced quarantine together, and if she was upset she could always ring down for John – get him to fetch her something. One of those pink drinks, or a little cake, or a fruit salad or something, if she was getting worried about her waistline. Better not mention her waistline. He laughed.

'You're looking lovely, Tilly. Never better. Give me a twirl.'

He looked at his hand – pale and wrinkled from the water. He had been in the pool a long time. It seemed all he did these days was walk around the hotel waiting out Tilly's sulk, swim endless laps in the pool, and wait for John to set them up with their little candlelit meal on the terrace. Same every day, menu getting a bit simpler now. John arriving, with the tray, or just the tray, or just the phone, appearing there, and John, impeccably discreet and nowhere to be seen. He'd reached out for the phone, but it had been dark and his hand was wet, and they were both too hot, the sheet tangled around his arm. Was that her problem? The phone? It wasn't a breakages must be paid for sort of place. He should spell that out to her. He'd dropped the phone and it had fallen to the floor and it felt, in the end, like too much to bother with. No need to fuss with the details, he'd decided. This was supposed to be a time of rest and relaxation. The phone handset rolled somewhere under the bed and Tilly didn't ask for the doctor again.

He felt someone touch his arm.

'No, not in there.'

He touched his bare chest. His skin was warm. Hot, even. Burning up. And he had been assiduous with the sun cream. A fair man like him couldn't be too careful. But standing there in the dark, the lights up here not working either (the lift on a different circuit, it must have been) he started to wonder if maybe she had not, after all, had a point. A point, perhaps, about the doctor, and getting hold of room service on the hotel phone. He remembered the noise she made – half whimpering, half coughing, the phlegm bubbling in her throat – and remembered that last thought, about how she wasn't pretty any more, not his wife, not the one he'd guided down the steps of the sea-plane with a proud hand in the small of her back, or the one who'd rolled her eyes and blushed when he'd picked a flower from one of the big bushes outside the hotel and tucked it into her hair, or the one who had whispered, furiously, about him making too much of a fuss when he'd sent her entire five courses back and ordered again because she'd took one look at his and changed her mind.

'I'll ring now,' he said, looking at his empty hands. 'Fear not. I'll do it now.'

She must have everything, must his Tilly. The whole world, he must take it and buy it and drop it at her feet, every single shining trinket – for how else would he ever be able to repay her for the miracle of wanting him all to herself? That wife – his own lovely wife – well, she wasn't pretty any more. She was, he would admit it now, remembering her sticky eyes, her swollen neck, the weeping cracks in those lips of hers, pretty unwell; and he himself, he felt how hot his own skin was and understood he had a touch of the flu too (stands to reason, the two of them shared everything – every coin and scrap that belonged to him was hers now – and the virus too, had passed between them as though they really were one flesh) though he (he reached for the phone, or had a thought about reaching the phone, or remembered a thought about reaching for the phone – one or the other of these) was still a believer in mind over matter. They could put that on his gravestone, he joked or had thought about joking or had decided after the fact would have been a good sort of joke to make at the time – to cheer her up in her dark times, as he had promised to do – but either way, whichever one of these it was, she had not laughed. His new lovely wife was not pretty any more, and still, he loved her with his entire squalid and craven little heart. He made a note – he must tell her that in the morning, when they were feeling better. He dropped the phone and it rolled away under the bed or somewhere else out of reach, and it didn't matter because sooner or later a John would come anyway, and as he waited he heard the horn of the passing cruise ship: the low dull blast of it, felt the vibration of it in his chest – this calling for help, a crying out – it felt like love.

Terry wiped his eyes. Sentimental old sod. Sunstroke. And three or four too many of those nice little cocktails that kept appearing at his elbow. He couldn't be blamed. He was tired, that was all. And in a place like this, there was no need to explain yourself. Self indulgence was expected. He thought of the Johns out there in the dark on the terrace, waiting silently for him and Tilly to turn up to their table. They'd wait all night, if needed, invisible in the shadows, the infinite black bowl of the sea and sky lurking behind them, the horn of the pacing cruise ship. No need to feel guilty. What else where they there for? Reduced only to their training, they were fulfilling the function required of them, these Johns, whether they were actually required, or not. As he himself was, remaining faithfully as exacting a guest as he was capable of, in the present circumstances. No need to report in. To explain that he and Tilly were under the weather and probably would not be requiring their table, their meal, their music tonight. The Johns would understand. He pushed open the door of the room and as the bluebottles billowed out at him in a great black wave, he saw the two still and sticky shapes in the bed, the great big honeymoon bed it was, the best in the place for the hotel's last guests, he'd been told, and he understood.

Midsummer Eve

Simon Clark

"This, then, is my hymn of praise to the wonderful and frightening domain of synaesthesia."

Victor Barstow, Quiddity of Found Sound, *Jan-March issue, 2014*

What I had just revealed to Dianne worried her. In fact, worried her so much that I saw a flash of horror in the woman's eyes.

"This music," she said, "has that effect on you?"

"Yes."

"So... hearing the music can make you see things that aren't actually there?"

"No, that's just it, the people really *are* there. I see them, hear them..." My heart pounded as anxiety gripped me again.

She took a deep breath. "You see Victor Barstow and his family again? Here in this cottage?"

"Yes."

"Even though they died fifteen months ago?"

"Not died. Disappeared."

"The coroner's verdict was murder-suicide. The police believe Barstow killed his wife and children, then himself."

"That didn't happen. Listen to the music. Victor and his family will appear again, in this house, just as if they are alive… you'll see what they did on the night they vanished."

Dianne Martz had called in at River End, a cottage perched on dunes between dry land and ocean, to say hello to me and to check on my work, which was to recover Victor Barstow's music from the chaotic mess he'd left it in just before… well, what I now know to be an extraordinary incident that took place here on that June evening.

Dianne sat there in Barstow's *Midsummer Sounds Studio*, a bright, grand name for what was, essentially, a gloomy subterranean tomb of a chamber in the cellar. Dianne had arrived, all twinkling eyes, white teeth and happy smiles, a lovely woman, who had sunk every penny she had into forming Aural Arcana, a company that specialized in releasing cult records that were so removed from the music mainstream they might as well have gestated in a deep crater on the Dark Side of the Moon. Dianne had expected to sit down with me for a convivial chat in the little studio, which was lit by a single angle-poise lamp on a desk, and equipped with vintage reel-to-reel tape machines, while black cables (for the likes of microphones, speakers and so on) hung from wall pegs – those cables resembled black cobras in the gloom, rising up with a menacing air, threatening to spit venom into your eye before sinking fangs, glistening with poison, into your body. Yet instead of relaxing there with our coffees, listening to what I had painstakingly restored from masses of butchered magnetic tape, and enthusiastically making plans for the long-awaited première of Victor Barstow's now legendary epic, poor Dianne Martz had listened to my story of what had happened to me during the last few weeks. Meanwhile, her daughter sat out in the car, eyes fixed to her phone no doubt, as teenagers do when they don't want to pay house-calls to people they neither know nor are remotely interested in. Much better to FaceTime a friend, or drift through Twitter, or even just play a game or two.

Dianne put her cup down on the table; that formidable woman had clearly reached a decision. "Look, Martin, you're working non-stop. You're marooned in this place." She smiled, attempting to ease what had become a tense mood. "Miles from anywhere with only rabbits and bloody seagulls for company. That's enough to send anyone off their flipping trolley."

"You think I've gone loopy? Cabin fever? The isolated geek who invents imaginary friends?" Even though I spoke those words myself, the damn well cranky tone I'd used made me wonder if I had spent too long trying to glue Barstow's masterwork back together again. A bit like those restorers who go slowly nuts as they piece together smashed vases found in burial chambers.

Dianne spoke with heartfelt sympathy. "You've been hammering away at this project for months. When did you last speak to someone?" She smiled that gorgeous smile of hers. "Someone human, that is? Not gulls or seals."

As I rubbed the stubble on my jaw, I noticed how

worryingly my hand shook. Quickly, I brought the hand down again, hoping she hadn't noticed.

"When did I last speak to someone?" I leaned back in the swivel chair (the very same chair where Barstow had perched his bones to carve his spine-tingling music from sounds that he'd recorded amongst the prehistoric grave mounds that rose up from the meadow nearby). "The ASDA delivery driver last week. That's who I spoke to last. Hmm... I admit it, I've become a long-haired, stubble-faced, wild-eyed recluse, haven't I?"

"A shave would allow me to see that handsome smile again."

She held my gaze for a moment, before quickly glancing at the cables hanging down, as if maybe they had caught her attention by twitching a little in a menacing way, then she fixed her big brown eyes on me again. "Martin, I'm worried about you. Music is power. Music lifts our hearts, or makes us cry, or inspires us, or relaxes us, and it can be a wonderful soundtrack when we make love, but music does not open a doorway into the past to let you watch people being murdered."

"No, not murder. Something else happened here... something amazing."

"We will, at some point, not now though, discuss what you thought you saw—"

"Did see."

"Okay, okay." Her voice became softer. "Now, I want you to pack a bag. I'll take you to a hotel in Scarborough. Rest for a couple of days, mooch along the prom, stuff yourself with fish and chips, swill down some Tetley's bitter, then we'll talk again. Promise."

"Dianne, give me ten minutes. I'll play you *Yitten*... and I promise you this: you will see things. Extraordinary things."

But I'm running ahead of myself. I need to explain who Victor Barstow is, why he – and what he created – is so important. And I must describe the chain of shocking events that brought me here to River End, a sullen bunker of a place, standing all alone, as if that brutal landscape will hold the house captive to the day its roof falls in and its mean, little doors rot in their frames.

To the front of the house is the meadow that swells and blisters with Bronze Age burial mounds. There are so many graves that I found myself referring to what must be a bone-saturated field as 'Tomb Land'. To the back of the house, the beach, consisting of swathes of yellow sand and rocks so jagged they would savagely rip the guts out of any ship unfortunate enough to crash onto them. A river flows by the cottage to the sea, not in a permanent, deeply cut estuary; instead its waters haemorrhage in an ever-changing delta over the sands. The river is knee-deep and maybe five metres wide. Lying at the bottom are masses of round, white stones. They put nasty pictures into my head of the bare skull-bones of murdered children. So much so, I even poked some of those macabre boulders out of the riverbed with a stick, just to put my mind at rest by confirming that they weren't actual skulls, because I did wonder if erosion had robbed bones from the graves out there in grim, old Tomb Land.

And beyond Tomb Land, a cliff of dark-as-midnight rock rises as high as a four-storey building, which further conspires to sever this entire area from the outside world. The sensation, which has grown inside my own skull – and grown in a way that's almost pathologically morbid – is that the eerie landscape here has become a kind of wireless hub, linked to a massive reservoir of danger, and images of violence, and the ghosts of people who suffered so much and who have died in terrible ways – and this sensation gripped me, making me so anxious. I found myself worrying that the unearthly hub only needs to be switched on for it to release a torrent of evil, and images of horror, and murderous ghosts. And that vile torrent will have the power to terrify and, perhaps, even destroy us.

Yes, I agree, this is a grim description of the cottage and the landscape but imagine my day-to-day life here. Working alone. Eating at the Barstow kitchen table. Sleeping in the same bed where Mr and Mrs Barstow slept and where, during the witching hour, they kissed and tangled their limbs together as they made love.

So, there you have it: a place that on a warm, bright day might seem a coastal paradise. Yet in grim November, drenched by cold rain, River End becomes a lonely corner of hell indeed. No wonder, then, that the shining spirit in the vodka bottle offered me such intimate company.

But still I am getting ahead of myself. Okay, back to the reason why I'm here. That is because of Victor Barstow, a man who composed music that has the power to reprogram certain elements of our minds, perhaps even reconfigure our souls. Look at any photograph of Victor Barstow: you see a frightened man. You feel that he expects every camera and phone that has ever taken his photograph will violently explode, hurling out sharp pieces of plastic and metal and red hot fragments of battery that will inflict hideous gashes all over his face, puncture his eyeballs, split his lips... that's what I sense he is thinking when he looks so nervously into the lens. *That thing will hurt me. I'm in danger... I don't want my photograph taken...* Check out those photos: you just know what's going through his mind. In any event, these pictures do reveal what he looked like. Black hair, cut quite short, a long face, clean-shaven, dark eyebrows, but the eyebrows always drawn together as if he worries himself sick over some deep-rooted problem or other. One hundred and fifty years ago, Barstow could have been the perfect image of the TB-riddled poet, who is down to his last shilling and contemplating overdosing on laudanum to end his troubles forever. But, yet again, I'm starting the story of Barstow's life in more recent times. I need, as the poet once wrote, "to begin at the beginning".

We roll back the years to 1980: back to the Yorkshire town of Castleford. Victor Barstow is dragged into the world, bruised and bloody, by a strong-armed midwife using steel forceps. His parents work in a supermarket where they stack shelves for a living. Nothing wrong with that, of course; that's honest work – after university, I spent three years at Morrisons: my domain, pop and dilute – I was the lord of fizz and cordial. To this day, I can't go into a supermarket without turning the bottles, so that the labels face neatly outwards. See, we all have obsessions in life: mainly small ones. Not like Victor, though. His obsessions were as massive as the bloody Alps.

Barstow's father dies soon after the birth, so young Victor Barstow is raised, along with two older sisters, by his mother, who remains a single parent, slaving long hours at the supermarket. On Barstow's fourteenth birthday, his mother suffers a heart attack, requiring a triple bypass to keep her ticker going. Barstow experiences a bizarre reaction to seeing his mother collapse onto the kitchen floor, where she lay like a goldfish out of water, eyes staring, mouth opening and shutting, gulping for air. This caused young Barstow to stop speaking for two years. In fact, he did not utter any vocal sound whatsoever in that time. That's what family members claim. He, himself, never spoke about the time he was mute, which has a certain symmetry about it, you'll agree. Age sixteen, after experiencing some profound reconfiguration in his own head, he uses his voice for the first time, recording a series of vowel sounds onto his mother's computer. For months afterwards, he obsessively manipulates those two dozen or so sounds, speeding them up, slowing them down, adding echo, reversing the 'ah' 'ooh' 'ee' utterances, overdubbing, changing pitch until the sound of his voice became a sophisticated array of 'musical instrument' sounds and tonal notes. With this toolbox of noise, he creates an eight-minute-long piece called *Sounds: Part Five.* Parts one to four no longer exist and nobody, as far as we know, ever heard them. By all accounts, Barstow was excited by what he'd done. Never one to normally reveal emotion, he did begin to smile, happy to have created such an extraordinary composition.

This happy state of affairs was doomed, however. Soon the smile would be banished from his face again after Barstow shared the music with a friend by the name of Jason Charrow, who'd somehow pulled a few thousand quid together to finance a horror film. Long story short: Charrow makes film, with the pleasingly resonant title *My Anvil Heart,* bolts on Barstow's *Sounds: Part Five,* creates a cult-horror flick, makes a lot of money. Critics love the film, declaring the soundtrack's composer a genius. Fans agree, claiming that the music makes the film. In fact, they insist this gore-fest wouldn't be much cop if it wasn't for that soul-gouging anthem – one that also, somehow, manipulates what the viewer sees into a work of wondrous, yet terrible beauty.

Indeed, you guess correctly about what happens next: Barstow, as so often with these projects, isn't paid a penny for his astonishing creation. Barstow's mother then suffers another heart attack, loses her job, can't pay the rent. On the eve of eviction, Barstow hikes ten miles to where his so-called friend had bought a nice house in Leeds with the loot earned from *My Anvil Heart.*

Barstow, a shy man, with a dread of confrontation, does confront the little shit who ripped him off. Barstow pleads with Charrow: "Give me just enough money to pay the rent arrears."

Charrow slams the door in Barstow's face, then calls

the police. Thereafter, Barstow breaks a window and uses a shard of the glass to cut his own throat; cops arrive to find a figure that's red from head-to-foot lying on the driveway. Barstow survives, quits music, finds employment in a call centre; there he works quietly, his ears guzzling in the sound of customers' voices all day. He marries; along come two children, a boy and a girl.

Then something miraculous happens. Years after its release, *My Anvil Heart* appears on a video streaming service, discovers a new audience who clamour for more music by Victor Barstow. He answers the call... well... sort of; he sells his house, moves his family to River End, where he converts the basement into a studio.

After that, he spends months recording naturally occurring sounds: the murmur of the river, flowing through a meadow where Bronze Age folk buried their dead. He also captured the sigh of the breeze, and those screaming barks that foxes make at night. He recorded other sounds, too, that might not be considered entirely natural – mysterious, ungodly sounds – or so some believed.

Then he transferred the recordings to his computer where he worked his own brand of Barstow magic on all that raw material of fox cries, breeze, water cascading over rocks, and, as some will insist, the melancholy songs of the long-dead – all captured by the microphone as they shimmered up through ancient grave soil.

Barstow, meanwhile, retreated further from the world. People scared him. When he stood in a bus queue, he genuinely believed the man in front of him would turn around and savagely punch him, or that the shopkeeper would yell abuse, or the girl on the moped would run him down. Towns terrified Barstow. His heart would even pound with terror when the postie arrived at River End to deliver a letter.

As Barstow worked, obsessively manipulating what was essentially a chaotic hoard of sound bites, gradually shaping all those hisses, blips, clicks, drones, fox yelps into a symphony, he turned his back completely on society. A realm ordinary to us yet terrifying to him. Where streets pulsated with danger. Where every man, woman and child could become his murderer. The poor devil lived in utter dread. All of which reinforces our notion that this was a deeply unusual man – one who experienced that strange condition called 'synaesthesia' – where people see sounds as colours. When I was a child, I was on a paler section of the synaesthesia rainbow: if someone said 'Friday' I pictured the word 'Friday' as always having red lettering. 'Wednesday' was blue to me. 'Sunday', black.

Then, fifteen months ago, Victor Barstow and his family disappeared. One of his sisters, on calling at the house after hearing nothing from Barstow for a week, found the front door open, windblown leaves in the hall and sheep crap in the kitchen, where more exploratory members of the local flocks had freely wandered in and out of the house. The sister also discovered twenty large storage boxes filled with magnetic recording tape. The tape had been cut into lengths of precisely twenty centimetres. There were thousands of these pieces – in fact, exactly fifteen thousand two hundred and thirty-six, when I came to count them before starting my mammoth restoration job. Barstow had, it should be pointed out, composed his music on a computer; however, said computer, containing the master audio files, had vanished. Stolen by thieves finding the house unlocked after the Barstow family disappeared? Or, more likely, Barstow himself had disposed of the computer. This was consistent with the man's odd behaviour. After all, in his teens, he painted pictures in shades of very dark grey, which he would then chop up with scissors, just retaining two or three postage stamp size pieces, then chucking out the rest. Yes, he was *that* strange, and yet people who knew him found him endearing and extremely likeable, despite radiating waves of sadness.

All of which brings this report back to me again. Dianne's record company rented the Barstow house from the sisters (they wouldn't be able to sell River End for years, not until Victor Barstow was officially considered to be dead). Dianne hired me, a composer of electronic music (think Tangerine Dream mingling with the deliciously subtle harmonics of Elaine Radigue) to piece together that Humpty-Dumpty of a mess, because it soon became apparent that the only surviving copy of Barstow's new masterwork only survived in those fragments of magnetic tape. No backup copy existed, and as far as we know the only person to have heard the composition was Barstow himself. Therefore, I had to splice leader tape to those individual fragments, put them on a tape machine, then transfer whatever had been recorded there onto my computer. With the aid of artificial intelligence software, plus my own experience as a musician, plus trial and error and guesswork aplenty, I listened to all those fragments, then gradually began to reassemble them into a coherent whole – again, please recall a ceramics expert piecing together tiny fragments of an Etruscan vase that has been shattered into a thousand pieces.

So, picture a forty-year-old guy, getting a little too thick in the waist from lack of exercise; cut and paste into this mental image long, unbrushed hair that is light brown, bristling stubble on a chin, eyes that are vividly red and sore, a guy with an aching back from sitting hour after hour at a computer in a cellar, and you have the image of me, Martin Stainforth, as I slowly, painfully, obsessively restore Victor Barstow's masterpiece.

Dianne knows how long I've worked on this project, and the process I used to reconnect those one-second bursts of music recovered from the butchered tape. Which brings me right up to the moment, there in Barstow's studio (hardly changed since the day he left, apart from the addition of my computer and a case of ASDA vodka under the desk), when I lean forward, elbows on the table, look hard into her eyes – and let me tell you those brown eyes of hers shift from side to side now; she's clearly uneasy being here with that unkempt loon (the unkempt loon being me) as I say, in a demanding tone:

"You must listen to what I've put together so far. There are fifteen minutes of—"

"Not now, Martin. Pack a bag. I'll drive you to the hotel."

I stood up so aggressively the front of my right thigh slammed into the table, sending my cup bouncing away across the woodwork, splashing her chest with tepid coffee.

With a flash of anger in her eye, she began to rage at me, but it was nothing to do with the soaking: "You idiot! You should have told me to bugger off!"

Astounded, I said, "Why on earth would I say that?"

"Because you are a brilliant artist. You create your own music that's just so bloody amazing. But instead, you accept my piddling little fee to do rescue work on a pile of chopped-up tape." Rising to her feet, she folded her arms, then began to pace from one side of the studio to the other. "Martin. You are too good for this...this cut and paste job. You are really talented. Do you realize that?"

"But restoring Barstow's music is a dream come true for me."

"Well, it shouldn't be! You should be recording new albums of your own. That's why you should have bloody-well howled at me: *Dianne! Bugger off!*"

Speaking softly, trying to be persuasive, I said, "Just hear what I've recovered so far." I stood up and went to my computer. "Trust me, you will see... how can I put it? Visions. You'll see a vision of what happened to Barstow and his family.

When someone is concerned for their own safety, they always glance in the direction of their intended escape route: in this case, the basement steps. No doubt she intended to run up those steps before dashing back to her car. She wanted out. She wanted to drive away from River End, and away from me, the shaggy-haired loon with a crazy yarn about music that could transport you, as if in the company of Dickens' Ghost of Christmas Past, back through time.

"Listen to this...this miracle. Tell me if you see figures appearing, like they're real flesh and blood." The words spurted from my lips. I wanted to tell her a huge amount in the brief moments I had before Dianne fled. By heck, would she phone for an ambulance for me? Or the police? Or medics with a straitjacket and a hypodermic filled with old sleepy time?

As I spoke, not really sure if it sounded coherent, or even rational, my hand darted to the mouse, fingers trembling like crazy; nevertheless, I managed to click on the play icon beneath big, black text that spelled out that strange title:

YITTEN

"Dianne, this is a new breed of music. No one has ever heard anything like it before. You know, the shock of the new, like when Daphne Oram first played that Optical Synthesizer she invented, or those who couldn't believe what they heard when Delia Derbyshire released music built up from tape loops of sampled sound – this is music from the heart of the universe... or music that the dead in their graves hear for all eternity."

"Martin. My daughter is out in the car. I am frightened for her as well as me. So, it's best I leave now."

With that, she quickly climbed the steps, her feet tapping lightly against the risers as she went, no doubt her heart racing and expecting that I would drag her back down into the cellar by her bloody hair... *no, I like Dianne,* I told myself. *Never would I hurt her. Never!*

I tried to reassure the woman, calling after her, "There are wireless speakers throughout the house, and in the garden. You'll hear it as you go to the car... once you've heard its beauty... its power... you will see what I saw. It's as if a magic eye, hidden under the skin of your forehead, comes to the surface, and that eye can see into the past."

By the time she reached the stop of the steps, Barstow's *Yitten* had begun. The computer channelled the music around the house and to the weatherproof speaker that I had hung from a monkey puzzle tree in the garden.

I followed Dianne upstairs to the kitchen, where I discovered that she'd already opened the door to reveal the landscape beyond at dusk: the silvery brook winding down the slight incline from the cliffs, the dunes, the dozens of burial mounds that formed grassy domes in the meadow. The constant hiss of the surf played a duet with the music throbbing from the speakers, Barstow's sampled notes hinting at what the heartbeat of some unearthly creature would sound like.

The music – that incredible music that opens our secret eye – those notes filled the house, growing louder. Dianne, as she stood in the doorway, glanced back at me. No, not *at me,* but at something, or someone, else.

The music evolved into a bass drone, which slowly rose and rose through dimensions of sound to a beautiful place – an aural wonderland. A place where musical notes glowed with their own vivid colours. Had Barstow's microphone, laid upon soft grass covering the burial mounds, picked up eerie, ghosting melodies sung by dead men, women and children, lying embraced by dark grave soil? Did a haunting chorus flow from mouths long since deprived of lips?

Dianne stared over my shoulder at something that horrified her.

She was, I told myself, staring at a man of thirty-five or so, who carried an unconscious youth in his arms. The youth wore black tracksuit bottoms and a black T-shirt.

I called to her over a crescendo of chords that boomed with the spine-tingling power of a cathedral organ. "That is Barstow with his son. The son has been in a coma since he was ten years' old. Jonathan went to bed one night and never woke up again. Part of his brain died."

A woman glided out from the gloom, across the lawn and toward the doorway, hair black as crow feathers, her eyes blazing with what must have been a fusion of excitement and absolute terror. This was Jacqueline, Victor Barstow's thirty-six-year-old wife.

"We must do it now!" shouted Jacqueline. "Police cars are coming along the track. We've got five minutes, otherwise we'll be too late!"

Neither Victor Barstow nor Jaqueline could see us. Remember the Ghost of Christmas Past in *A Christmas*

Carol? Something like that happened here. We could see the Barstow family; they could not see us. I don't know if Jacqueline walked through Dianne, actually passing through her body, or had somehow walked past her. I couldn't tell for sure, but suddenly Jacqueline was in the kitchen, a small woman who made precise, darting movements.

She said to Victor: "Carry Jonathan outside. I'll see if Katy's ready."

Now the music turned in on itself – a series of melodic whispers, followed by sighs that descended in pitch from sky-high to a deep, deep sound – the respiration of a dinosaur sleeping in the shadows. That's how it seemed to me. In this strange place, a man as strange as Victor Barstow might have somehow caught an echo of that primordial beast's respiration from fossil bones found scattered on the beach.

Lunging at Dianne, I pulled her back into the middle of the kitchen.

"You see them, don't you? Tell me you can see Barstow and his wife and son!"

"Martin, let me go."

"You are going to witness everything."

"No… I'm taking Amber away from here." Her eyes glistened with tears.

"Be brave, Dianne. Look at Barstow… how gently he's holding his son. He is doing this for love."

Above the music, back through those long, dead months, that should have forever vanished into the shadows of what *has been*, the howl of sirens. And in the distance, the beat of blue lights as cars crawled along the narrow, twisting, difficult road that leads to River End.

But what, exactly, had triggered Barstow into embarking on this astonishing course of action? What I think motivated him was this: local kids had been giving Barstow a hard time by trying to provoke him. You see, they had decided that the musician was a 'complete nutter' (their words), so a bunch of youths would pelt the house with eggs, post dog crap through the door and shout insults at Barstow from the dunes. For bored kids this was innocent amusement – you know, make the looney run out of the house, shouting so hard you think he'd bust a gut. Yeah, all a good laugh, eh? The teasing became torment for Barstow, then nothing less than mental torture – this is what lit the dangerous fuse.

Jacqueline opened a kitchen drawer, then drew out a knife with a foot-long blade. A sharp knife, tapering to a vicious point.

My hand squeezed Dianne's arm tighter, a crushing force that made her yelp.

I whispered fiercely, "You see them, don't you? What is it in Jacqueline's hand? What will she do with it?"

"I can't see anything... and this damn racket is driving me insane!" With a scream of pain – either from that suddenly brutal drilling-into-concrete shriek blasting from the speakers, or my savage grip, I don't know – she wriggled free. Once out of my grasp, she staggered away, knocking over one of the table chairs as she went, and slamming with painful force against the fridge. Then she was outside, leaving the scene of Jacqueline with the knife, and Barstow carrying Jonathan.

I followed Dianne. After, that is, taking a knife of my own from the drawer. A knife with a murderous point.

The music played on – conjuring an aura of growling, prowling menace. The sound of wolves snarling as they close in on you, fangs glinting, predatory eyes burning in the gloom.

Picture the scene: white surf rushing in over the beach. While blowing in from the North Sea, a cold breeze, its invisible claws gouging and tugging at dune grass before making the wild flowers in the meadow writhe as the blast of air assaults them – the winds animated the landscape: bushes, trees, grass in constant movement. Our surroundings had indeed come to life – or so it seemed to me on that awesome evening when Barstow's greatest creation, his torch song without words, flowed from the speaker that hung from the monkey puzzle tree. Dark clouds flew overhead, somehow driving brutal images into my brain of panic-stricken refugees, trying to run from their enemy – an enemy with a lust for massacre pulsating in their hearts. Barstow's music does that. The notes, those soaring harmonies, followed by bass notes plunging deep as a grave, have the power to conjure disturbing visions within your brain.

I followed Dianne, knife gripped tight in my left hand, steel blade flashing to the rhythm of the music. Dianne ran to the car, threw open the driver's door, then turned to look at her daughter in the back seat. Amber cried out, an expression of absolute alarm on her face. What words she shouted at her mother I do not know, because *Yitten* grew louder. An immense volume that would have drowned thunder.

The breeze gusted harder, harrowing the grass on ancient grave mounds until it seemed as if those grave mounds expanded and contracted, the same movement as a beating heart, laid bare by a surgeon's knife.

And the Barstow family continued their preparations. Victor Barstow, still carrying his son, emerged from the house. Jacqueline, armed with a knife, pausing in the doorway, called back indoors.

"Are you ready, Katy? It's time we were going."

Those words called to tardy offspring are pretty much the same called out by any parent to a child when it's time to head off to school or to see Grandma. Not tonight, though. Those words throbbed with another meaning entirely. *It's time we were going...* I knew where they were going, because I'd seen these events a dozen times before whenever I heard Barstow's composition, and the alchemy of its notes released images that had once been held captive in some other place, maybe in the fabric of the landscape, or even in another dimension.

I walked toward where Dianne stood by the car. She fixed those bright, frightened eyes on me. I could almost hear the terror-struck pounding of her heart.

"Martin." She pointed at me. "Far enough... don't come any closer."

"Tell me you see Barstow carrying his son. And there's Jacqueline. What's she holding in her hand?"

"There's nobody else but you... you with that damn knife!"

"What about those flashing lights? That's the police. They'll be here soon."

"There are no police cars."

"No, not in our time, but those cars are the ones that arrived at River End fifteen months ago. The reason they came here is all down to Barstow's teenage daughter, and what she did... she found three Swedish tourists pitching a tent in the dunes, close to the house. That would have spoilt everything. Ruined the family's plans. Because as soon as the campers saw what was happening, they would have called the police. Katy, however, persuaded them to camp further away down the coast, insisting that the tide would wash into the tent. They believed her, but when one of the Swedes came back... he'd left his phone on a rock... Katy flew into a rage, believing their scheme would be thwarted. She pulled a knife on the tourist, slashed his arm. Of course, he fled back to his friends and they dialled 999... that's why police cars are heading toward River End... the road, as you know, is nothing more than a dirt track, so they can only move at a crawl... look... Katy is coming out of the house now, fastening her coat. You see, Barstow's fear of society has infected them all. They are all determined to escape society somehow... to leave behind this world that frightens them so much."

Dianne gave a helpless shrug. "Martin, I don't see Barstow and his family."

"You lie because you are too scared to admit to yourself that the music unlocks a vision of what happened here."

Dianne's eyes locked onto the knife: that sharp blade

had the dreadful power to hypnotise her, to capture her gaze, to force her to stare at what she feared might become a murder weapon.

With a deep breath, she wrenched her gaze from the knife. Then she moved with explosive speed, hurling herself into the car behind the steering wheel, and activating central locking. That done, she began talking quickly to her daughter. Amber responded by firing what I assumed to be questions at her mother, perhaps questions in the vein of: *"Who is that lunatic? What's he going to do to us? Why don't you start the car and just bloody-well drive!"*

Dianne, however, lowered her window by a finger width so she could call out to me above the demon howl of *Yitten*: "I'm going to get help for you, Martin."

"I can't let you go."

"So you're really going to murder me if I don't stay?"

"This isn't for you." I raised the knife. "It's for the tyres. I'll puncture them to stop you leaving."

I moved toward the front tyre on the driver's side, getting ready to push the blade's sharp point through the rubber wall. With all the tyres flat, the car would be stuck here. The sandy soil of the drive was so soft the car would quickly bog down, even if she tried driving away on flats.

"Martin... you win! I'll come with you. Just leave the tyres, okay?"

Dianne, when she opened the door, murmured something to her daughter in the backseat. At that moment, I could not hear what was being said.

I soon found out, though. When Dianne exited the

car, Amber sinuously poured herself from the back into the driver's seat, where she sat anxiously gripping the steering wheel while staring out at her mother, clearly wondering what the hell would happen next. Maybe the flash of a knife, her mother staggering backward, blood jetting from a gash in her throat.

Dianne's voice was calm. "Martin. I'm coming. Just please dump the knife, okay?"

By way of answer, I threw the knife into the bushes.

Diane managed a smile, one of genuine gratitude. "Thank you."

I glanced at Amber; she hadn't started the engine, but did sit there, one hand on the steering wheel, the other hand out of sight, probably gripping the ignition key. *Amber's sixteen,* I told myself, *can she drive?* But then Dianne taught both her son and daughter to play musical instruments and to speak Italian before they even hit their teens, so she had probably taught her daughter the rudiments of how to handle a car. Amber sat there, no doubt ready to power away, just in case I went berserk or retrieved the knife.

Meanwhile, the music had evolved into a series of sighs – the most mournful of sighs – the sound people make when standing by the bed of someone they love, who has just drawn their final breath.

Dianne asked, "What now?"

"We follow the family down to the beach."

"Why? What do they do there?"

"You'll find out. Remember *My Anvil Heart*? Victor Barstow composed the film score. Lots of people who saw it believed—"

"Believed they saw different versions of the film to other people who'd watched it. There are theories that the music reconfigured electrical patterns in the viewers' brains, triggering hallucinations."

"It goes much further than that." We walked side-by-side to the beach now. Ahead, three figures moving with calm determination, the largest figure carrying the unconscious youth. "Several people watching *My Anvil Heart* report that after hitting pause, to grab another beer or whatever, they opened doors in their house to find characters from the film either standing there or enacting earlier scenes. In fact, several people report waking up at night to see the schoolteacher character from the story rushing around their bedroom, screaming until her head explodes, just as it happens in *My Anvil Heart*."

Dianne moved ahead of me now as we passed through narrow gaps in the dunes. By this time, twilight had deepened, stars were beginning to appear. A meteor scratched a line of white fire across the sky. Even though the gloom had thickened, I plainly saw the family just ahead of me, as they trudged across the sand. Ocean scents filled the air, while a cold breeze tugged Dianne's hair back from her face. And, yes, I still heard the music, even though the house was some distance away. In fact, Barstow's music no longer appeared to emerge from the speaker in the monkey puzzle tree. Instead, those haunting sounds flowed out of the landscape – the sand, the boulders, the meadow. The world around us appeared to channel Barstow's composition that was so beguiling, surprising and, without a shadow of a doubt, terrifying. Terrifying, yes, because those notes had an occult power – a power to reach into my brain and plant frightening thoughts there.

I asked: "What do you see now?"

"Sea. Beach. You. Nothing else."

"The music will unlock images. Victor Barstow carrying his son. Daughter Katy, linking arms with Jaqueline. The family love one another so much. There is complete trust. Ah, I never noticed that before. Jacqueline has thrown away the knife."

Dianne took my hand, a signal to stop and look at her. "No, Martin. She still holds the knife in her right hand."

"Then you do see?"

Dianne nodded. "I pretended I didn't in the hope you'd come with me and leave that bloody awful haunted house."

I looked into her face, one that I'd grown so fond of, and wish I could... oh, you can guess, can't you? What I wanted to happen between Dianne and myself? I don't have to tell you wish-fulfilment love stories of what might have been. Though I cannot stop myself from spinning rosy fantasies in my head, of working in the studio on my own music, then welcoming Dianne at the end of the day, with glasses of wine for both of us before making the evening meal.

"Come on." I spoke gently. "These must be the final moments now. We can go up close to the family. It's okay. They can't see us."

Dianne froze – she must have guessed that Barstow's

family would, in the next few moments, die a horrible death on the beach, and Dianne feared that she would see every bloody detail.

She whispered, "What happens? Does Barstow kill his family?"

"I haven't seen any further than where we're at now. I only spliced the final five minutes of *Yitten* into the master copy today."

"So, you don't *really* know what they did?"

"No."

"Are you telling me the truth? Will they die?"

"Believe me, I don't know. Before, when I played the recording, and saw what you've seen, I got this far, then the music stopped and the vision, for the want of a better word, just vanished right here."

Meanwhile, Barstow's anthem to God-knows-what continued. There would be five more minutes of that extraordinary, transformative music. And those additional five minutes would reveal the family's fate.

Dianne glanced back at the flashing lights, growing brighter and brighter, as police vehicles approached River End. "They're almost here."

"Remember, we're seeing the cars from fifteen months ago. They're not really here – not today anyway."

Now, hand-in-hand, we approached the little group on the beach: mother, daughter and father glancing at each other with such fondness. They were as close-knit as any family can be. Three people linked by invisible bonds that are unbreakable. The son, Jonathan, appeared to be peacefully asleep in his father's arms.

Shingle crunched underfoot as we drew closer to the family. Strands of brown kelp lay scattered over clusters of blue-black mussel shells. A starfish gleamed in a rock pool of dark water, seemingly in imitation of the North Star burning bright above our heads.

And the music continued. Entering heart and brain and blood and soul... the tonal masterpiece that Victor Barstow had pieced together from recordings of those sounds he'd captured, then manipulated on the computer. For example, he would snip out a micro-second of a gull's cry, then multitrack that cry a thousand-fold before slowing it down in order to create a massive pulse of sound – and through it all he wove the mysterious sighs he'd recorded when he rested the microphone on those ancient burial mounds.

Victor Barstow, holding his son lovingly to his chest, spoke to his wife and daughter: "I have already told you this, but it's important you hear it again." His voice possessed a musical quality in its soothing tone. "When I made good progress in the studio, I'd transfer what I recorded to my phone so I could listen to the music on my headphones as I walked through the meadow or along the beach. You already know that *Yitten* allowed me to see what happened to the people who lived here five thousand years ago. A peaceful, happy tribe who made their own clothes, grew their own food, and caught fish with nets they wove from long strands of ivy. But then a fierce warrior tribe attacked the people who lived here. I called the warrior tribe the Outlanders. They were vicious. They ruthlessly massacred entire populations in order to steal their land. That's what they did here. I saw them with my own eyes as I stood in the field next to our house. The music transported me back five thousand years and I saw the killers arrive with their spears and axes, and they viciously drove the people from their huts. Those that resisted were murdered. A few dozen survivors fled into the forest. In a sense, what happened to them has happened to us. We have had our lives ruined by that vile gang that keep attacking our home and destroying our happiness and our peace of mind. To my horror, I realized that the eternal menace that is always present in the outside world had come to hurt us, just as it came to destroy the lives of the peaceful people who had once lived here." The music surged louder, investing his words with such a solemn dignity. "Yet something marvellous happened. A miracle. Those peaceful people from long ago, those who survived the massacre, found a way to escape the invaders. They knew the ocean would protect them... so they all decided to surrender themselves to the water, where they would be transfigured. After that transformation, they would continue to live in peace – though now their lives would continue in the new world of the sea."

"That's what we're going to do, isn't it, Dad?" The teenage daughter spoke with real force. "That way the bastards who are making our lives hell will never hurt us again."

"That's right, Katy. Tonight, there will be a marvellous transformation. We will be safe. Nobody from the outside world will ever interfere with our lives again, or hurt us, or make us miserable."

"We will be happy." The mother smiled. "It's just a case of believing strongly enough."

The daughter touched her brother's face, a tender gesture of affection. "And Jonathan will be alright? He'll be with us?"

"Of course he will."

Barstow nodded in the direction of the house. "The police are nearly at the end of the track. We can't put this off any longer."

The family moved toward the sea, which had turned from dark green to black – black as liquid night.

Dianne and I followed. We didn't hold hands now, but we repeatedly glanced at one another, each knowing what the other was thinking. When our eyes met there was reassurance enough there. And I know I derived comfort from the way she looked at me.

Then everything changed. The past few moments had been almost serene. Now, however, the music soared: louder, louder, louder... an enormous surge of aural menace, ranging from shrieking screams to violent crashes of thunder. Following that, a tremendous bellow that could have been the sound of a god, writhing in agony as they, after a billion years, died a searingly painful death. The speaker in the monkey puzzle tree couldn't possibly discharge such a monstrous quantity of decibels. Once again, I could only surmise that ground, sea and air had become the conduit for Barstow's creation, the symphony that had the power to shatter the golden spires of heaven and extinguish the fire pits of hell. Not so much music but the distillation of the experience of birth, life and death of everyone who had ever lived.

Pulsing blue flashes signalled that the police cars had reached River End. Barstow reacted with horror.

"Hurry," he called to his family. "If the police see us, they'll ruin everything."

The family hurried toward the bone-white surf as dusk became night. The music soared higher and higher until Dianne clamped her fists against her ears, trying to prevent those jabbing thrusts of sound from driving spikes of pain deep into her skull.

"Follow them," I shouted to her. "We've got to see what happens. We must know what they did!"

"They went into the sea, that much is obvious." Her eyes were screwed up, the music inflicted such pain on her now. "We don't have to see what happened – we know! They went in, they drowned themselves."

"But we can't be sure. Come on."

I grabbed her elbow, part guiding, part shoving her after the Barstow family who approached the cold ocean, which seemed to become ever darker and more forbidding.

Then we were no longer alone. More figures streamed across the beach – men, women, children. Many carried babies in their arms. Those running people wore primitive clothes made from woven strips of wool, animal skins. Some carried baskets made from tough dune grass. Panic and fear and terror blazed from their eyes. These were the Bronze Age folk that had once lived in their little wooden homes on the coast here: the same peaceful tribe that Barstow had just described, and who had laid their dead to rest in burial mounds in the meadow.

"The music," Dianne shouted with a mixture of horror and awe. "The music has brought prehistoric people into our time."

"Or we've been shunted back five thousand years into theirs."

We followed the Barstow family, who were now just twenty metres from where the tide rolled in, drowning the beach.

Then I understood the cause of the villagers' terror, because here they came: a swarm of warriors – they flooded over the dunes before fanning out across the beach, pursuing the adults and children who fled in the direction of the sea. These warriors were the Outlanders. The brutal invaders who had murdered so many of the tribe that dwelt here, before driving the survivors into the forest. Though where these survivors could flee to, Heaven alone knew. There was simply the ocean in the direction they were running, nothing else: no miraculous causeway they could pass over to an island fortress, no boats waiting to carry them away to safety – no, only the cold, impassable barrier of salt water trapping them on the beach where their enemy could slaughter them.

The Outlanders raced across the sand, whooping with excitement. They were armed with bronze-headed axes, bronze-tipped spears and heavy wooden clubs. Soon they ripped into those fleeing people – hacking, cutting, stabbing, mutilating. Axes chopped away arms with a single stroke. Spears punctured hearts. Bronze daggers opened up bellies, spilling blue intestine out, as if their victims' stomachs had opened red mouths to vomit blue snakes.

A warrior, with a huge mane of black hair, pounced on Barstow, felling him with an axe blow that cut down through his right shoulder as far as his rib cage. The boy in the coma flew from Barstow's arms and went rolling across the sand in a loose flapping of arms and legs, face still expressionless, his eyes as firmly closed as the deepest of sleepers.

When the axeman raised his weapon, ready to smash the blade down into Victor's skull, Jaqueline used the knife she'd brought with her from the kitchen. With lightning speed, she slashed the blade across the back of the axeman's knees, shrewdly cutting through vital tendon and muscle that keeps a human standing upright. The axeman fell. Instantly, daughter Katy picked up a pebble as big as a melon and delivered such a fierce blow that the stone smashed the bones in their attacker's face. He yelled out in agony, the guttural sound of a wounded brute.

I realized that three time periods had fused together there on the beach, the once impenetrable barriers that separate past from present being dissolved by the incantations that Barstow had, by pure chance, given voice to in his music.

Proof of this came when Jacqueline suddenly turned to Dianne, fixed her powerful stare on her, and said, "Whoever you are, help us reach the sea."

Dianne stared at Jaqueline in amazement. "You can see us?"

"Of course I can. I saw you in the house, only I pretended I couldn't because I thought I was going mad – oh! That doesn't matter now. You must help us reach the sea. Only the water can save us now... the change will take place there."

Puzzled, Dianne shook her head. "What kind of change?"

The question went unanswered because just then, an arrow let loose by an invader embedded itself in the beach just centimetres from my foot. I reached down, gripped the shaft – one that was hard and real in my grasp – and pulled the arrow from the sand. The flight was made from bird feathers; the arrowhead, of greenish metal, possessed wicked swept-back barbs. The point must have been honed against a rock until it was as sharp as a surgeon's scalpel. Clearly, the arrow was no hallucination, no chimera: it was real. Deadly. A missile that could kill.

A female warrior, aged twenty or so, barefoot, with a sunburst pattern of blue tattooed lines radiating outwards from her nose, drove a spear into the back of a young woman who fled toward the sea, carrying a toddler of perhaps fifteen months, the little child wrapped in a piece of brown cloth no bigger than a sheet of newspaper. The young woman, her spinal column severed by the spearhead, fell dead-legged and paralysed onto a scree of limpet shells, the young child wailing as it struck the ground.

The warrior finished the young woman by jabbing the spear into her throat, then savagely twisting the wooden shaft, enlarging the wound, severing arteries. When the warrior was satisfied her victim was dead, she turned her hard, malevolent stare to the infant, crying for its mother.

Dianne pounced. She flung herself on the warrior, a muscular figure that radiated aggression, hatred and sheer bloodlust. Dianne gripped the warrior's mane of raven hair in both hands and succeeded in keeping that rage-filled woman off-balance. Katy immediately dragged the spear from the warrior's hands then she returned a favour – driving the dangerous point of the spearhead into her throat, as Dianne held that fierce creature by the hair.

Katy withdrew the spearhead from the throat of what was now a corpse, not even appearing to notice the way a thick, treacly blood, nearer black than red in the gloom, dripped from the spear onto pale sand. Katy, flinging the weapon aside, darted to the weeping child, picked it up and murmured gently until the child stopped sobbing and cuddled deeper into her protecting arms.

By this time, Jacqueline had helped Barstow to his feet, his clothes sopping wet from blood that gushed from the ugly wound in his shoulder.

Victor looked at me with an expression so grave that shivers ran up my spine. "Help us, Martin."

"You know who I am?"

"I saw you in the house... thought you were a ghost..." The man grimaced: the axe wound must have been pure agony. "You appeared in the studio whenever I worked on my music."

"I was no ghost, Victor."

"No. You were the man who unlocked the magic in *Yitten*. It was you who achieved that marvellous effect, not me. You were the genius..." Barstow swayed, blood loss draining him of life now. “Hurry… not much time left.” His sad gaze turned toward his son, who lay on the beach, forever trapped in that death-like oblivion. “Victor. Please save my boy.”

I picked Jonathan up: he was surprisingly light – in fact, he seemed to have no weight at all as he lay there limply in my arms, his features smooth from never having known anxiety or heartache or pain since that dreadful night the lights of his cerebral cortex went out.

The sea itself seemed to illuminate our world now, its waters possessing a strange luminous quality, turning the ocean into a glowing turquoise. The sharp freshness of the beach at night filled my nostrils, while the breeze delivered a cooling caress to my face. And the music grew louder, becoming much more than sound now – instead, those great, long notes with their cathedral organ power resonated with the kind of energy found, perhaps, in that vast Black Hole which lies in the heart of our galaxy. The music didn’t so much as fill my ears – it became a new kind of blood that flowed through my veins, filling my heart and surging into my brain, releasing emotion that I’ve never felt before.

The Outlanders had stopped their slaughter now. They had to, because their weapons no longer had any effect on their intended victims. What’s more, the slaughtered men, women and children rose to their feet, their wounds miraculously healed. Slowly, they walked down the beach and into the sea. As waves foamed around their ankles, then knees, then hips, they lifted their arms up until their hands were higher than their heads, then they sang out to their gods of sea and earth and life and death. The villagers moved without any sense of fear or urgency now. And within moments all I could make out were the rounded shapes of their heads against that turquoise glow, and then, one-by-one, the heads, every single one of them, sank beneath the surface and I could see them no more.

Caught up in this strange, dream-like effusion of events from bygone times, I carried Jonathan into the waves. Jacqueline helped Barstow, who still bled from the axe-wound, which unlike the wounds of the Bronze Age villagers had not healed. Why this was so I don't know; perhaps his cut flesh hadn't repaired itself because he lacked the firmness of belief in the ancient gods of those ancient people – whatever the reason, the crimson gash in his shoulder yawned wide, revealing the whiteness of exposed bone, while the wound discharged a cascade of liquid red into the brine where it formed dark blooms that expanded in waters that possess the same concentration of salt as a human tear.

Katy, still gently embracing the little child wrapped in his scrap of blanket, waded through the surf.

For a moment, the Barstow family paused, chest-deep in rolling waves that seemingly tried to push them back toward dry land, as if testing their resolve. However, they did not retreat and so, at last, the ocean relented. The backflow of water began to ease them outward... out where there would only be cold liquid beneath their feet, not sand. I carried Jonathan out to his mother and father where, with smiles of gratitude, they took their son from my arms and, between them, floated him away into deeper waters. It was at that point the gaping axe wound in Barstow's shoulder changed – pink flesh began to fill that deep gash; the bleeding stopped, exposed bone vanished beneath moist pinkness: there must have been some healing force flowing through this corner of Yorkshire after all, and it had repaired Barstow's injured body.

They moved further and further away from the shore, until they became dim shapes against that shining turquoise of the ocean. And, finally, I could no longer tell mother, father, daughter and son from the rolling waves, and that is when I realized they were gone.

We sat out on the beach all that night, Dianne and I. So close, my left arm pressing intimately against her right arm. I don't recall us speaking to one another. The physical closeness made speech unnecessary. Eventually, the music had stopped, and the symphony that replaced Victor Barstow's last masterpiece was the symphony that has been endlessly played on repeat here for thousands of years – this was the melody of the sea as the tide turned once more. An ageless music accompanied by the whispering chorus of the breeze and sobbing cry of gulls. When Barstow's music fell silent, the debris of battle, including the two corpses of the Outlanders, had disappeared, just as if they were no more than images painted in water that had slowly dried and vanished.

So, when police cars and an ambulance tentatively

approached us across the beach, led on foot by Dianne's daughter, who pointed at us with the phone she held in her hand, there was no sign of what had happened last night, and absolutely no visible residue of those events. We were in the here and now again. The present once more sealed off from the past. The sun shone down on the beach, the greenery of the dunes emerald bright and the sky turned from pale grey to blue.

The women in the green uniform of the ambulance service put warm blankets around our shoulders before helping Dianne and I to stand. Police officers asked questions, gently but firmly. However, we were too exhausted, too emotionally drained, to answer in any meaningful way.

Amber put her arm around her mother, helping the paramedic guide her to the ambulance. At some point, one of the police officers must have snapped handcuffs onto my wrists. I don't remember when they did that, or whether I resisted in any way. I was only half awake at that point.

I do remember, however, one female police officer pointing at objects in the waves. These rounded objects possessed bright eyes.

"Look at those," she said in astonishment. "I've never seen so many seals before. There must be hundreds of them. And they're all watching us." She shook her head, marvelling at the spectacle. "Look at their faces. They look almost human, don't they?"

Midsummer Eve

Aliya Whiteley

There will, eventually, be darkness.

'Are you thinking of marrying him?' says my auntie.

'I'm merely in it for the sex,' I tell her.

'Thank goodness for that! I don't think he's the marrying type.'

The formal garden is peaceful, bathed in the last light of the longest day, and I choose a red rose to cut from the bushes. I like to catch them at the perfect moment, just past the bud but not quite yet in the act of advertising. I bend and twist the stem until it breaks, and I strip it of its thorns, breaking each one off in turn, letting them fall to the grass. Maybe they'll stick into my auntie later; she will potter around this place in bare feet. Well, one bare foot. The left. She wears an immaculate pink dress, with a sash tied at the back, like a little girl taken to a tea party. The right foot is encased in a silk slipper bearing grass stains. But the left foot is always out on display, the big toe turned inwards, the bunion standing proud.

'If I wanted to, I'd marry him.' I don't like the idea she's picked up that I'm essentially unlovable. Perhaps it's a deflection. I don't think anybody ever loved her.

'Is that for me?' she says shyly, ready to curtsy and accept her rose.

'Absolutely not. You shouldn't be out here too much longer. Go in and get ready for bed.'

Her shoulders slump, and she wanders away: not towards the house, but around it, taking up her usual circles. She and I both know that the night won't come yet, and there's much still to do.

In the hall sits my love, on the bottom step of the grand staircase, his elbows on his knees, his palms pressed together as if he prays. I've never thought of him as the praying type before.

He looks up and says, 'It's you.'

'It's me.' I cross the chequered floor, tiles of black and white, to reach him. He shifts on the stair so I can squeeze in between his reassuring body and the banister. I'm soft, small, compressed. I love the way he makes me feel like a celestial object viewed through the wrong end of a telescope. I realise I will marry him, if he asks. At this moment.

He opens his pressed-together palms and gives me confirmation that he wasn't praying – see, I do know him – but holding something. It's sitting in his left palm. A silver ring.

I hold out the rose.

He takes it in his right hand, as if weighing the two objects. Then he focuses his attention on the folded heart of the rose, where the smallest petals curve and come together. It reminds me of my baby, who emerged in silence, as red as the flower and open-mouthed in aghast wonder. She was folded up tight too. It took her hours to uncurl.

'Do you remember?' he says.

'Absolutely.'

'And then there was the thing with the—' He can't tame the words, but he doesn't need to for my benefit. I laugh at the memory, and he laughs too.

The ring still sits on his palm.

I would look at him under my lashes, and ask for it, but all I can think of is my auntie and her coquettish ways that have stuck to her so long after she should have shaken them off. *Is that for me?* So I don't mention it, and he doesn't either. The light of the sun streams through the long windows. I have so much to do, but I can't move from him, not yet. I want him: his laugh, his memories of me, his ring.

I put my head on his shoulder. He hums a familiar tune. If I'm using him for sex, I'm not doing a good job of it. But I want to imagine I am, so I say, 'Meet me upstairs for a quickie?'

'Really?' he says, his eyebrows raised. I've managed to surprise him. He acts as if I've never propositioned him before, and that annoys me in its erasure: that time in the car, that one trip to the seaside, in the dunes. He's meant to be storing all these events for me.

I sit up straight. 'You don't have to, if you're too busy.'

'No, I want to, sure. A quickie. Tell you what, take this and I'll see you up there.' He holds out the ring.

'Are you sure?' I ask him.

'Just to hold on to,' he says. 'For now.'

I take the ring and I put it on. It fits. But it doesn't mean what I thought it would mean. I don't feel different.

He plays with the rose, touching the petals that are already curling back from the centre. The beauty of it will soon be lost. At least a ring is permanent; I think I've got the better deal. But it's also true that nothing lasts forever. Not even today. The night will fall and I'll be in bed with my lover – that's the promise we made, which has nothing to do with rings and roses.

I stand up, and abandon his clarity. 'See you later,' I say, as casually as I can, and I take the stairs to the next thing that must be done.

Here lies my baby, not quite asleep, because there's only so much blackout blinds can do. She's drowsy, though, even with that slice of light sneaking into the nursery, cutting its way across the foot of the cot.

I lean over the bars and whisper to her, words that make perfect nonsense: *it's the tone of voice that's important,* someone said to me, once. It feels like old wisdom, which is the kind I like.

She meets my look with a grave glance of her own, but I see no recognition in her filmy eyes. Of course, she's too young for that: we have to make our memories. Who knows what will become her first memory? My own is of this very room, lying still, watching motes in sunlight. That meandering drift of a thousand specks, like microscopic creatures in a sea. I was adrift amongst them, my only company. Nothing can ever quite feel real in a nursery.

I want her first memory to be a good one. Better than mine. Not a memory of loneliness. If only there could be a guarantee that she'd catch and hold my face in her mind, at just the right moment, full-blown in the act of loving her.

'See this face?' I tell her. 'This face will always take care of you.'

She crumples up her eyes and mouth at the sound of my voice. Oh, don't cry, don't cry my baby. She doesn't cry. I'm relieved although I know, objectively, that she must cry sometimes. It's part of the process. It causes me pain, though, and I'm so sick of pain. The thorns that get scattered underfoot.

She settles once more. My beautiful one. There will never be another thing so perfect in this world; at least, not to me. Not today.

I slip off the silver ring and place it on her chest. She's so tiny, she can't grasp it, can't even open her fists yet for long. The ring sits between the buttons of her sky blue baby-gro. What will she give me in return? Love? I long for it, but I can't be sure. That's not how the world works, and I can't remember loving my mother, not as a gift to meet her expectations, nor as a trade for her time. Children are so selfish.

In the absence of anything better I take a toy from her cot. A stuffed rabbit. It's small and soft, it's one of many such toys that are lined up alongside her, and it feels good in my hands. I press it to my face and breathe in the smell of her that has sunk into the material. She won't even know it was hers to begin with, if I claim it now. It was one of the many presents that arrived in the first days after her birth. So many boxes came, the cards inside addressed:

To Mummy and Baby

These aren't our names, I thought, with every envelope I opened.

'I'll take care of this for you,' I tell her. 'I'll do a good job of looking after it. I'm a responsible adult now.'

She doesn't move. Her eyes are closing, closing, closed. I think she's finally about to sleep. I tiptoe away, determined not to wake her; there's nothing as delicate as the senses of a baby. Just one sound, and she'll stir and then I'll be stuck here all night, singing all the same old songs. But no, I've made it to the door and I can move on to my next task. There are still so many things to get done.

My gramps can always be found in the billiards room.

I confess I don't know the rules for billiards; in truth, I've always resisted the information, thinking it might spoil the magic of watching him play. He lines up his cue and strikes the white ball so that it hits the black, and the black travels at a sedate, slowing speed to the corner pocket where it sinks. He turns to the rack on the mantelpiece, beside the clunky carriage clock, and slides the pointer along the numbers to record his score. He only ever plays alone: *you make the best competition for yourself*, he once told me.

'Unexpected maintenance,' he says, as he chalks his cue. 'It's falling down, one piece at a time. A quote for the roof, remind me, and tree surgery, that's necessary. Trees and their growing and dying back. It's not the branches you need to worry about as much as the roots, though, disrupting the foundations.'

'I'll remind you,' I say, knowing it'll never stay in my head. It doesn't matter. I can't believe this house will ever fall down, no matter how he worries.

'Bunkins!' he says, his sharp eyes falling to the stuffed rabbit. 'I remember Bunkins from when you were little. You wouldn't be parted from him. Where did you find him?'

'Upstairs. In the nursery. But he's not mine – he's brand new.' It comes to me – I've left the ring on my baby's chest. How could I have been so stupid? I'm a terrible parent, she could swallow it, it could stick in her throat, she could somehow manage to pick it up or roll on it or I don't know anything, anything, I've failed to protect her from herself, I must get back to the nursery and make it right—

My gramps reads it all on my face: 'Now, now, now, what's wrong, my little one?' He puts down the cue and comes to me, folds me up in his arms, and he's right. I am still the little one with a stuffed bunny in my hands and tears in my eyes for a hurt he thinks he can take away.

'I'm a terrible...mother...' I tell him, in between sobs, and he strokes my hair and says, 'We're all terrible people in lots of ways, angel, not to worry. Not to worry.' He wraps me up in the smell of cough sweets and wood shavings; why should he carry such scents on him? I don't understand how age impregnates the body and changes it all for its own purpose. And in the middle of that thought I realise that my guilt has lost it sharp edge. My need to return to the nursery and retrieve the ring is passing. It's funny how quickly the worst emotions, born of the most painful mistakes, leave us. Perhaps that's what age is – the quiet adjustment to the weight of blame.

My gramps lets me go and steps back. He looks long into my face, and I into his. His assessing eyes are almost lost in the folds of his face, but not quite. Not quite. I wonder what he sees.

'There now,' he says. 'That's better.'

'It is,' I say. 'How did you do that?'

'It's the tone of voice that's important.'

He's right again, of course. It's the softness that age brings to his voice, so easy to mistake as wisdom.

'I made you something,' he says, as he returns to the billiard table and picks up his cue. 'It's on the sideboard.'

Yes, there's a new object on the long table beside the mantelpiece, where the framed photographs of the long family line are kept, white faces schooled into serious poses amidst the grey of the past. It's a little wooden cross, crudely made, but varnished so it shines. Is that why my gramps smells of wood? I picture him hard at work on this for me, cutting and planing and measuring his work.

'Thank you,' I say. 'I'll cherish it.' I put down the stuffed rabbit and take up the cross. It's rough, and lighter than I thought it would be.

'Good good. Get along, then,' he tells me, and I do as I'm told, even though I hate the next obligation. Still, what can be done? It must be completed, and I've never failed in my duty. I pocket the cross, and set off for the cellar.

Down in the cellar, down where the sun can't go and the wine that can't be drunk is racked and numbered, lives my twin.

'Oh god,' she says, when she hears my footsteps. All is dark until I light the candelabra, waiting in the usual alcove for me, set back in the damp bricks. The light throws long shadows over her face, her white body that twists away from me. She is so very ugly.

'I hate this process as much as you do,' I tell her, and she says, 'I very much fucking doubt that.' It's better when she swears and shows her anger; it makes it easier to turn the wheel, so I get on with it, and crank it round, pulling at the spokes until the rope around her hands tightens, and stretches her out upon her rack. She screams. She uses terrible words, awful words. How I despise her. How grateful I am that she's decided not to beg for mercy this time.

'Come on, come on,' I mutter. It's become my mantra in this place. Let time move on, let this be done, but she won't give in easily, she won't submit. I put all my effort into the wheel and strain, strain, until – there. A crack. It's not loud but I feel it through the spokes, and I know my job is done. I let the wheel go and step close to look at her body, dangling upon the rack, the fight in her spent.

She's naked apart from one shoe, which she has always refused to give up. A silk slipper. I suppose she clings to the idea of walking out of here. Well, don't we all.

I search for the new injury, and find her skin has split in the hollow under her ribcage. A clean line across her white stomach. No blood.

This bit is always the same. I have to check. I put my fingers to the wound. She's the same inside. Just the black. She winces at my touch, and sucks in her breath. 'No,' she says, 'No no no,' and I tell her gently, 'I have to.' I reach inside, and probe the darkness. Empty. There is nothing inside her. Nothing at all.

I remove my fingers. 'Done,' I say, and she breathes out. The cut will have healed by the next time I see her, forming a fine scar. She has so many of them, all over her torso, her face, her limbs, her hands and feet. I have tortured her everywhere.

'Oh god,' she whispers, again. She's big on god; perhaps that's the prerogative of those in pain. I remember the cross I carry, and I pull it out.

'It's a present,' I tell her, and she says, 'For me?' so eagerly that I can't bear to tell her no, no, it's my present, from my family. I stand on tiptoe and put it in one of her hands, stretched high above her head. Her fingers fold around it with such delight, even though it means she can't see it, can't ever put it down. It will grow heavy, surely. Still, we cling to what we must.

'You look terrible,' I tell her.

'Isn't it getting dark?' she says.

'Surely. It's Midsummer Eve, but it will get dark eventually. It has to.'

'It always does.'

It's good to end on a note of agreement. I would leave it there, but as I walk away she calls out, 'Bring me something from the garden next time, won't you? Please? For old times' sake.'

What harm could it do? I'll cut something fresh, something sweet and summery, so she can be sure of the time of year. I try to fix this task in my memory, but there are so many tasks to get done, and the night is close now. It's coming. I'll never get everything done. But I could go now, to the garden, and get it done. Sooner is better than later. I blow out the candelabra and leave her behind me. I'm awash with the relief of the hard task done properly.

I cut through the empty living room to avoid the hall and climb out of the window to reach the garden. In the distance I can see my aunt dancing, twirling, her head thrown back, her hair loose. She thinks I'm unlovable, but she's wrong. I'm certain of it.

She's in the formal rose garden, so I'll have to speak to her, and have another one of those interminable conversations about my life choices. If I'm lucky it won't last long. The light is dusky and intense; surely these are the final moments before sunset? I set off at speed, half-running to reach the roses. So many tasks to get through, but even Midsummer Eve will end and leave so much undone. Still, I must believe that there will, eventually, be darkness.

C.C. Adams
www.ccadams.com

Jenn Ashworth
www.jennashworth.co.uk

Simon Clark
www.nailedbytheheart.com

Stewart Hotston
www.stewarthotston.com

Rachel Knightley
www.rachelknightley.com

Stephen Laws
www.stephenlaws.com

Lisa Morton
www.lisamorton.com

Linda Nagle
www.liberatetutemet.com

Robert Shearman
www.twitter.com/shearmanrobert

Kelly White
www.kellywhite.co.uk

Aliya Whiteley
www.aliyawhiteley.wordpress.com

blackshuckbooks.co.uk

Also available:

GREAT BRITISH HORROR 1:
GREEN AND PLEASANT LAND
FEATURING STORIES BY
JASPER BARK
A.K. BENEDICT
RAY CLULEY
JAMES EVERINGTON
RICH HAWKINS
V.H. LESLIE
LAURA MAURO
ADAM MILLARD
DAVID MOODY
SIMON KURT UNSWORTH
BARBIE WILDE

GREAT BRITISH HORROR 2:
DARK SATANIC MILLS
FEATURING STORIES BY
CHARLOTTE BOND
PAUL FINCH
ANDREW FREUDENBERG
GARY FRY
CATE GARDNER
CAROLE JOHNSTONE
PENNY JONES
GARY MCMAHON
MARIE O'REGAN
JOHN LLEWELLYN PROBERT
ANGELA SLATTER

GREAT BRITISH HORROR 3:

FOR THOSE IN PERIL

FEATURING STORIES BY

STEPHEN BACON

SIMON BESTWICK

GEORGINA BRUCE

KAYLEIGH MARIE EDWARDS

JOHNNY MAINS

PAUL MELOY

THANA NIVEAU

ROSALIE PARKER

KIT POWER

GUY N. SMITH

DAMIEN ANGELICA WALTERS

GREAT BRITISH HORROR 4:

DARK AND STORMY NIGHTS

FEATURING STORIES BY

G.V. ANDERSON

SIMON AVERY

M.R. CAREY

PAUL M. FEENEY

KATH DEAKIN & TIM LEBBON

ALISON LITTLEWOOD

MAURA MCHUGH

PRIYA SHARMA

PHIL SLOMAN

CATRIONA WARD

REN WAROM

Lightning Source UK Ltd.
Milton Keynes UK
UKHW010731210721
387515UK00001B/45